A tingly sensation dancing through my heart wakes me up. I roll over and look at the clock—3:13 a.m. It's finally happening! Tomorrow night, the musical *I wrote*, is premiering at school. But it's more than that. It's my chance. By the time the sun rises, butterflies are turning cartwheels in my stomach. My whole life is about to change…

Believe

"*Believe* is a magical, incredible, and fiercely honest off-the-grid middle grade adventure. Take a deep breath on page one because from the very first sentence to the last, you'll be on the ride of your life with Kristi Kate, a moxy tweenager who has no doubts about who she is, where she's going, and the perfect outfit to wear on the way! Just try to put it down once you start."
—JENNIFER GRAESER DORNBUSH, Speaker, Author & Screenwriter for *God Bless the Broken Road*

"The adventurous, precocious, and ever so talented Kristi Kate captures your attention within minutes. Her childlike spirit combined with her intuition, maturity, and sense of self, will have you soaring through the pages. *Believe* is a must read for young girls!"
—MYRA GALE MONROE, Founder of Gracious Role Models and Speaker for Inner City Youth

"Kirstin Leigh captures the voice of her characters and her writing is filled with hope. These are two good recipes for readers to keep coming back for more. Particularly an audience of young people who need to find stories of hope and faith lived out authentically in a very chaotic world."
–TERRY BOTWICK, Lightbridge Entertainment, former President of Big Idea Productions, and Vice President of original programming for The Family Channel

"Readers are immediately swept away by the heart and mind of Kristi Kate, a vivacious twelve year old who refuses to let go of her dream. Leigh's characters and settings are so vivid, you feel you are with Kristi Kate every step of the way. Full of suspense, readers will race through the pages of *Believe,* an uplifting journey of dreams, disappointments, and discoveries."
–SHARON FIALCO, Author, Producer, and Publisher of the *Starabella* Series of audio musical books for social sensitivity

Ephesians 2: 7-10, The Message: The Bible in Contemporary English. Copyright © 1993, 1994, 1995, 1996, 2000, 2001, 2002. Used by permission of NavPress Publishing Group.

Jeremiah 29:11 is taken from the New International Version of the Bible. Copyright © 1973, 1978, 1984, International Bible Society. Used with permission.

Summary: "A vivacious twelve year old wants to prove to the world—and her dad, that she's more than just a dreamer, but when an emergency landing in her family's small plane leaves her with no way of making it home in time for her own musical debut, she's challenged to see past her shattered hopes, and discovers the purpose inside her dream."

Subjects: Fiction/friendship/family/relationships/God dreams/music/talent/church

All rights reserved.
ISBN-13: 978-1721220915
ISBN-10: 1721220917

Author photo: compliments of Michael Hevesy

What do you do when your dream is bigger than you?

Ella Grace
Always Believe
in your Dreams

Believe

Love,

KIRSTIN LEIGH

Kirstin Leigh

For God

Thank you for Believing in me. For trusting me with this life-changing project. For giving me the passion and the discipline to turn a "God dream" into a reality, and the faith to keep Believing.

This book is also dedicated to my
mom and sister, Kimber

You took this project—and me—to another level. Thank you for reading, encouraging, editing, laughing, praying, and creating with me. I love you more than all of the superlatives, adjectives, and fantabulous words in the world! Together, there is nothing the three of us can't do.

Special thanks to

Carin Hining and Leslie Whitman Smith for your insights, love, and editing advice.

My niece, Louise Emmi Delgado for cheering Kristi Kate on from the start. You are a true artist, and God has big plans for you.

Judy Blume for creating characters who became my "best friends," inspired me to dream big, and to always be myself. (Even when I didn't know who that was yet.)

Robin Zarzecki, Michele Williamson Luksic, Traci Wynn Henry, and Velvet McGriff, for always being ready for an adventure.

For my new friends who have
just picked up this book

You are special. You are not alone. Your Dreams are real. And the whole world is waiting for them to come true...

✶✶✶ 1 ✶✶✶

I Kristi Kate, do solemnly swear that from this day forward, I will listen to the entire sentence—not just the first few words, before I get excited. Before I jump up and down, before things like "shopping at The Unique Chic Boutique" alter my judgment, and especially before "YES, YES, YES" pops out of my mouth.

I close my diary and lay my head back. If I had done this today, I would have heard the "Dad has some business in that area and offered to take us" part of the sentence. Dad flies a very small four-seater plane and I hate flying. Yet, here I am. Scrunched up and uncomfortable, with my seat belt pulled so tightly across my chest, I can barely breathe.

If my mind hadn't been so busy with *tomorrow*, I would have known something was up. Mom would never drive four hours to go shopping, even if it is supposedly where stars shop. (In all fairness, she didn't make me come. But when I accidentally said yes, her eyes lit up. She always wants us to do things as a family, and it rarely happens. I didn't want to be the one to disappoint her.)

"It's going to be fine," Mom says, startling me out of my misery.

"Fun?" I question, my ears popping. *This is the absolute opposite of fun.*

"Fine," Mom repeats.

I mentally add one hundred exclamation points to my "from this day forward" entry. For now, I'll just keep my eyes closed and focus on... the fact that I convinced the school board to let the third and fourth graders perform in a musical I wrote! I still can't believe they said yes. Granted, I've spent every afternoon for the last three months with nine and ten year olds, but…it's been pretty awesome. And, I have a secret. I'm making my singing debut.

The reason my debut is a surprise is because I didn't want to ask if it would be okay. They (as in Mrs. Wright) might say something like "that's way too much pressure for a twelve year old." And then I'd have to explain that "Pressure" is having songs in your heart and nowhere to sing them. And that twelve is a number, not my age. *I really hope everyone likes surprises.* I *actually hate surprises. But the rest of the world…*

Ugh! This little bitty plane is shaking its way through the clouds—pizza for breakfast was not a good choice. And clouds are such a false advertisement. Gazing up at them words like soft, cuddly, and peaceful come to mind. Going through them is like a battlefield. Dad's assured me a million times that "the plane is not falling apart." He says the bumpiness is due to the change in pressure or gas or something. I'm sure he's right (he's really smart about those things), but it doesn't make them any less nauseating. "Are we almost in Atlanta?" I ask, burying my head into my pillow and holding my stomach.

"Almost," answers Mom.

We live in Nashville (Georgia, not Tennessee). Atlanta's the closest city, and while it's not New York or Hollywood by any stretch of the imagination, a lot of television shows are filmed there. I could possibly be discovered. That's why I have on my Signature Outfit. ("Signature" is a style you're known for. Not that anyone actually knows me right now—but still.) The pink sweater has perfectly fake fur around the collar and sleeves, and it goes with a hot pink skirt that flares out at the knees. I fell in love as soon as I saw it. Mom on the other hand—

"You have nowhere to wear that, Kristi Kate."

"That's exactly why I have to have it." Mom gave me her I'm-listening-even-though-I'm not-sure-I-want-to-hear-this look. "I need to see it every day, so I can visualize my future— where I have countless places to wear it."

Mom contemplated. "Visualizing the life you want for yourself is important."

Yes!

"But I'm not paying a penny for that outfit."

And that was that. So I pulled out my babysitting money and bought it myself. I look at it as an investment. If I look like a star, it will be easier to be discovered. *I don't know if it's the wind or what, but it feels like…*

"Ahh!" Mom gasps—then immediately tries to cover it up with a cough.

Without my permission, my eyes fly open. I don't see a big city, I see a big lake! And a weird looking sidewalk and tons of trees. "Where are we?!"

"Quiet!" yells Dad.

Mom reaches back and puts her hand on my knee. "Everything's going to be okay," she whispers, as the plane fights with the air.

I squeeze my eyes shut, pray as hard as I can, and hold Mom's hand so fiercely it might fall off. (And she doesn't tell me to stop, which scares me even more.) I put my other hand over my mouth and bite the insides of my cheeks—half on accident and half on purpose. I don't trust myself not to scream and… *Ahhhhh*, the plane jerks to the right and to the left. We bounce up and down, and just when I think I can't take any more…*BOOM!* The wheels pound to the ground. We skid back and forth finally S - C - R - E - E - C - H - I - N - G to a halt.

"On ground," Dad exhales into the radio.

Static and silence fill the plane. The radio people are supposed to respond, but the static's getting louder. I force my eyes open and "Ahhhhhhh!!!!" We landed on the SIDEWALK I saw from above!

Dad slams open the door, takes two steps, and turns around, "Where's my phone?"

Mom gently un-pries her hand from mine and starts opening up compartments, "I'm not sure." Dad grabs his jacket off the seat—his phone falls out. He snatches it off the ground and stomps off. "Thank God we're okay," Mom breathes. "I'll be right back," she says, hopping out of the plane.

"What? Where are you going?" I shout, to the back of Mom's head. "And where are we?" Mom doesn't answer me. Probably because she doesn't know! After a few more minutes of freaking out, I realize it doesn't matter. We just survived an almost plane crash for goodness sakes. *Dear God, thank you for…* "Oww!" a nasty mosquito just bit my neck. *Buzzzzz Buzzzzz…* I aim, swat and *Bam!* Knock myself in the face. That's when I realize I'm about to suffocate. By the time Mom and Dad appear, my gratitude is almost nonexistent. I'd like to ask why they left their only daughter locked up in a broken airplane on the middle of a sidewalk, but the heat's holding my vocal chords hostage. So I just sit here (with my pink outfit melting into my skin).

Mom has her "everything's fine" face on. (It looks so good on her most people never question it. I don't question it either—even though I don't always believe it.) Dad's glaring at the plane. I wonder what it did wrong.

Come to find out, the radar detector compass

thing that is supposed to tell you how to get places, had a malfunction. And this, along with visibility issues (whatever that means), is why we landed on a SIDEWALK—which supposedly, even though there are no other planes or people around, is actually an airport in ALABAMA!

So much for shopping and getting discovered today. The good news is Dad can fix anything. When he isn't at work, he's building and fixing things in the garage. It's why he's always "too busy." *I will never complain about this again.* "How long will it take you to fix the radar detector compass thing?" Dad studies a manual and takes a few tools out of the emergency box. "Will we be home by five? Brianna and I are…"

"That's enough!" says Dad.

I don't know why he's mad at me. I didn't land this plane in Alabama. "Excuse me, please."

"What?" my parents snap in unison.

"I have to go to the bathroom."

Mom wipes the sweat off her forehead and points

to a shack. "The tower's locked." *What tower?* "And there's nothing else…"

"I'll find something." Mom shrugs her shoulders and lets me go. Guess they were really getting tired of not answering my questions. *Now what?* I pick up a long stick (it just seems the thing to do), and push my way through the weeds. If all this grass were sand, I'd think we had landed on a deserted island. The water is ultra-blue, there's even a roped off swimming area. Maybe it's a camp! A camp that looks great in the brochure, but when you get there, you realize the brochure was it. (This has never happened to me, personally. But it did happen to a girl in one of my favorite books—and everyone knows that all good stories come from some sort of experience.) Meanwhile, it's like someone just decided to throw out some concrete, make a long sidewalk in the middle of nowhere and call it an airport.

"Can anyone hear me?" I shout. Almost like the world's answering me, I hear a car or… I push the annoying, tall grass aside, and… it's a bus. And a girl with long, dark hair is leaning out the window singing. I wave my arms like a crazy person. "Hey!" One of the kids spots me and starts laughing. "Is there a bathroom around here?"

"Over there!" yells the girl from the window. "Look over there!"

I think she's pointing to a tree that's mostly hidden by the bushes. Oh, well. In my mind, this is going to be the airport's official bathroom. "Thank you!"

"I love your skirt," she shouts as the bus speeds away.

"I love your hair," I shout back. I forgot I was wearing my Signature outfit. I must look really ridiculous. She didn't say it in a sarcastic, making fun of me way though. Maybe she thinks I'm a famous actress filming a movie here! That would make this entire scenario make complete sense.

Meanwhile, since nothing or no one is anywhere in sight, I make my way to my newly found bathroom.

✶✶✶✶✶✶✶✶✶✶✶

"Sorry I took so long. Where's Dad?"

"Did you find a bathroom?"

"Yes, Ma'am."

"You did?" Mom asks. "Where?"

I motion to an area in the distance. Mom opens her mouth but nothing comes out. "I really had to go, there was no way…"

"Your dad's calling some friends."

You've got to be kidding. "Can't he wait until we get home?"

Mom's face twists and turns. "He's trying to find a place for us to stay tonight." Mom waits for me to say something. I'm waiting for her to tell me she's joking. We stand that way for what seems to be a very long time. "There's a slight possibility we won't make it back in time…"

"No!" I scream not letting her say it. "I have to be there. I'll walk. I can hitchhike!"

"Honey…"

11

"This is my chance! You have no idea how hard it's been. Ms. Smith is the only teacher who even likes me. I don't understand, if this is an airport then..."

"It's not a commercial airport it's a..."

"I'll take a bus! I just saw one."

"You're not taking a bus," Mom says, almost as upset as me. "And it's not that your teachers don't like you. They just dislike that you don't always go along with the rest of the class."

"I don't know why Mrs. Wright got so upset. As soon as she saw my acting book hiding behind my history book, I immediately told her I'd already read the chapter they were studying last week. And to prove it, I showed her how I'd taken the test at the end of the chapter." *Why am I even thinking about this right now?* "I was doing what you always say to do—using my time wisely."

"Yes, I know," Mom sighs. "I don't think it worked out so well."

"If I could just go to a Performing Arts School..."

Mom gazes at the nothingness we're surrounded in, "I'll talk to your teachers. Surely they'll understand."

"No, they won't. And what about my students? I promised Brendon I'd be there to mouth the words in case he forgets—he's never even been on a stage! Tabatha's great but she forgets to focus. I promised I'd remind her. And Jasmyn didn't even want to be in the play because... No one is coming to see her, Mom. Not even her own family. I promised I'd be her person..."

While I'm telling Mom about every student, I start hiccupping. All my words are coming out in pitchy syllables. Mom can't even understand me... I can't understand me. And I'm hot. I'm so hot, I might pass out.

"Come here." Mom says, wanting to hug me.

"I'm getting in the water," I hiccup.

"You can't..."

I wait for her to tell me about the snakes, crabs or whatever else lakes in the middle of sidewalk airports might have in them, but all she says is, "That's your favorite outfit."

"I don't care," I mumble, moving toward the water. *I care so much.*

I swim to the rope. Back and forth. Over and over again. The cold water is making my brain feel better. But every time I come up for air, I see disappointed faces. On accident, I start to cry—this makes my nose fill up with water and I start coughing. Which underwater, doesn't feel too good.

*** 2 ***

"I have a plan," Dad states confidently, not even commenting on the fact that I'm drenched.

Yes! My heart jumps. *We're going home!* But, no.

"Joe… you remember Joe, right?" he asks Mom. Mom nods, like she's trying to remember, but doesn't. *Who cares about Joe!* "Well, Joe's grandmother lives here," Dad continues. "She's out of the country, but said we could stay at her house."

This is his plan? "What?" I cry. Dad tells me to "cheer up" then picks up his phone and disappears. I hate it when people tell me to cheer up. Obviously, if there were any way to be cheery I would. Half the time people are like, "Why are you always smiling?" Then the second you don't—Bam! Un-cheery. And seriously. Right now? Cheery?

"Looks like we're walking," Dad says, returning from his phone call. Under his breath, he whispers something to Mom about the number his friend gave him for the taxi service being disconnected. Imagine.

After swatting off a million bugs and nearly stepping in quicksand, we finally find an overgrown path that leads us to the rickety street the bus was on. Gigantic trees swing back and forth in an intense rhythm, casting eerie shadows on the street. This is the perfect setting for one of those scary movies Mom technically won't let me watch.

Mom must be thinking what I'm thinking, because every few seconds she turns around to check on me. Probably to make sure some madman hasn't kidnapped me or something. Maybe if I did get kidnapped, the kidnapper could drop me off at my show. *I wonder if my parents would pay a ransom thing.* Somewhere in the back of my mind, I laugh. I should add "has a sense of humor in crises" to my resume (when I get one).

After we've walked about a million miles, Dad pauses to check his phone then points at a moss covered, rectangular shaped something. "That's it over there."

Oh. My. Gosh. It might have—at some point, resembled a house. But the thing I'm staring at looks like an abandoned... I don't know what to call it, but it's surrounded by weeds that go half way up to the roof, and "Are you sure this is it?"

"Yes, I'm sure," he answers, annoyed that I'd even think to question him.

Since I'm practicing the art of thinking before I speak, I don't point out the obvious. We're in Alabama—not shopping at The Unique Chic Boutique, and not on the way home, so you could be wrong! It's good I'm working on this, because it wouldn't have gone over well. (And if I *were* kidnapped I'd need him to pay the ransom.) A legitimate question would be *what kind of person leaves their house unlocked?* But my mind answers my question before I get it out of my mouth. *The kind of person who lets strangers spend the night.* Plus, who would break into a house that looks like this anyway.

The door creaks as Dad pushes it open. I stand back, half expecting someone (or something), to jump on us. What I don't expect is... it's beautiful. Talk about outward appearances being misleading. This house should wear a sign: Don't make assumptions about me! *Maybe I should wear a sign...*

I have to admit, if it weren't for such horrific timing (and the almost plane crash), I would totally see this experience as an adventure. An adventure I might star in one day! This room alone is a vision of my future. I don't know what I like better—the crystal chandelier dangling from the ceiling, that it's so spacious and elegant (too much furniture gives me a headache), or the spiral staircase that's calling my name. I debate for a second. Then I walk gracefully up the stairs, like I would if I were in a movie. I wonder which room I should go in first. *I wonder if I should go in at all.*

My legs are obviously faster than my decision making skills, because by the time the thought registers, I'm already inside—and I've never seen anything like it. The walls are soft pink with iridescent sparkles running through them. (Not tacky sparkly, just the perfect amount of dazzle sparkly.) White lace curtains flow from diamond shaped windows, and right in the middle of the room is a round canopy bed with pink, hot pink and lavender satin pillows thrown on top. This room belongs to someone glamorous. Someone who dares to be different and... I have to meet her. And I can't wait to see what's next.

Wow. At first, I think someone pasted pictures and passages from books on the walls, but when I get closer, I realize that they're actual letters—some dating back to the early 1900's. They're addressed to a Delilah. *The Grandma!* There are pictures of her dancing, swimming with dolphins, skiing, jumping out of a helicopter, playing with tons of kids, accepting awards... I've never seen so many exotic locations and people. She looks different in each picture (she must be like 100 now), but she's easy to spot. It's her eyes. I don't know what it is, but… *I want mine to look like that.*

The next room is a little boy's. He has one of those beds that look like a car, except it's a train. It sits a couple inches off the ground and instead of having drawers like the ones I've seen, it has a built in train station. I've never seen so many trains, not even in a toy store. Then again, I haven't been to a toy store in years, and I've never been to the boy's side.

I flip on the light switch to get a better view and *Ding!* a train track comes up from the floor. One track leads into a forest with dinosaurs and other wildlife animals. Another route takes you into a city full of lights and Hollywood action. *Choo Choo*, a wide gate opens and the trains ease their way out of the station. Some take their time, like they're deciding where to go. Others race ahead. I've never been impressed with boy's stuff, but this

is awesome. *I wonder what this other switch is for...*
"ROAR! TWEET, TWEET!" Answer is—a jungle.

"What's that noise?" Mom shouts.

Where is the switch that makes them go back to the station? Found it. Note to self: Don't flip switches in wonderfully strange houses. "Mom, wait till you see these rooms!" I say, running down the stairs.

"Is that where you've been—snooping around the house?"

"I was looking for the bedrooms. We have to sleep somewhere."

"That's true. We also have to eat." Mom opens the freezer. "What looks good?"

"Has Dad found out about the part? Because Brianna's parents could come and get me." (Brianna's my BFF.)

"I didn't think they were back yet."

"Oh, yeah," I remember gloomily. "How about Tristian?" Mom gives me a look. I pretend not to know what the look means. "Tristian, Brianna's brother, he stayed at home, and..."

"I *know* who Tristian is. I also know he has a permit—not a license."

"But..."

"I don't care how great Tristian is. I don't care if he's been driving since he was five. I do not, under any circumstances, want you riding with him. Understand?"

"But what if it's an emergency?" *Like this is.*

Mom's eyes lock with mine. "Not even in an emergency like this."

She read my mind.

"Is there any food around here?" Dad asks, walking in. Before Mom can answer, he casually adds, "The parts will be delivered tomorrow morning. Should be home by mid-afternoon."

"Are you serious?" I exclaim.

"If things go like they're supposed to," he nods.

I purposely ignore those last few words and throw myself in his arms. "This is the best news ever." Dad pats my back, then picks up a magazine. *What is wrong with him?* Anyway. There won't be any disappointed faces tomorrow. I'll be there, just like I promised. *And when he sees me on stage...*

"So," Mom smiles, "what would you like for dinner?"

"We could call Dominos," I suggest happily.

Mom laughs. "I don't think Dominos delivers here."

"They might. Who would have thought this amazing house was on the inside of what from the outside, looks like a falling apart, un-kept, haunted house?"

Mom has a that-didn't-sound-very-nice look on her face, but she doesn't say anything. (Probably because she's thinking it too.) "Maybe..."

I know there's not a Dominos anywhere near here. But I love that she said maybe—there's always a possibility. "Or," I open the cabinet, "I could have spaghettios." I bet the Grandma got the spaghettios for the little boy with the train set. I make a mental note to mail a can of spaghettios to this address as soon as I get home. (I wouldn't want him to come to visit and not have his favorite food.)

Meanwhile, Mom is setting the table—like she would do at our house if we ever ate together. This is definitely not the family outing she was hoping for, but Mom is all about looking at the positive.

By the time we sit down, Dad's already eating, but this doesn't stop Mom. "Dear God, thank You for this food, and thank You for giving us a safe landing today..." *Though I'm ultra-grateful for this, it would have been better if we had landed in the right place. Aaah! Why is it so hard to concentrate on the grateful part?* "Thank You for friends and strangers who are giving us their home tonight. Please remind us to do the same for others, and give us a safe trip home tomorrow morning. Amen."

"AMEN," I proclaim.

Mom tries to make small talk, but Dad's in a mood. He should have seen that something was wrong during the pre-flight inspection. He didn't tell me this. *I just know.* Mom finally gives up and takes the dishes into the kitchen. For some reason, I feel bad for him. "Sorry I was kind of a brat earlier." Silence. "You can tell your friend that I think his grandma's house is spectacular."

"Glad you won't miss your thing," he says, not looking up from his plate.

"Thanks, me too." He has no idea what my "thing" even is. Much less what it means to me. "You're coming, right?" I think he nods—or maybe he's just chewing.

"You okay?" Mom asks, as I walk into the kitchen.

"How could I not be? My show is back on," I smile, avoiding her eyes.

"And it's going to be fantabulous."

"Dad's coming, right?"

Mom hands me a dishcloth. "He said he was."

After Mom and I finish the dishes, I venture into the grandma's, I mean, Delilah's room. I don't want to go to sleep yet, but I definitely don't want to *think*

anymore and her room is full of distractions. I feel a little like I'm trespassing. Like a kid tagging along on an adventure I wasn't completely invited on. But she did say we could stay here. And if she knew me, hopefully she'd invite me over herself. (She's definitely not someone who'd let the difference in our age—almost thirteen, and possibly 100, stand in the way of a good friendship.)

Above the bed, is a picture of a very handsome man gazing into Delilah's eyes. I carefully climb up to get a better look. *I wonder if Luke will ever look at me like that.* Luke is fourteen, and plays baseball with Tristian. I've secretly been in "like" with him since the first time I saw him—which was exactly eight months ago. That's also when I knew that one day he'd be my boyfriend. And I'm not one of those girls who drool over every guy who walks by and plans their wedding twenty years in advance. I might not even get married—but probably I will. I'm definitely going to kiss Luke one day. Anyway, it took him four months to notice I existed, and another couple weeks to say more than "Hey." But now, we're...

"What are you doing?" Mom asks, walking in.

"Nothing."

Mom moves around the room, taking in the pictures and letters. "What a unique woman."

"Where do you think she is right now?"

"Somewhere nice," Mom says, scooting me over. "I thought you were sleeping in the pink palace."

"I am, but... Is that rain?"

Mom nods. "I haven't heard rain like this in a while."

"What's that horrific noise? It sounds like a baby groaning or...."

"Probably a cat in heat. Or a tree owl."

"A tree owl?"

"Maybe it's a coyote," Mom says, offhandedly.

"Coyotes are real?"

"Of course, they're real."

"Do you think there are bears out there? Or lions? I mean, we're in the middle of a forest, staying in this strange yet amazing house." *This is weirder than I let myself realize.* "Aren't you the slightest bit scared?"

Mom points to a very intense man walking into the woods. "See that man in the picture?"

"What about him?"

"It was a bad winter. Family had been stuck in the house for days. He was afraid they'd starve. He didn't want to do it, but…"

"Do what?" I interject.

"The wind was brutal. Snow was blowing so hard he could barely see. He knew his daughter wouldn't eat meat, so he captured frogs disguising them as…"

I throw a pillow at Mom. She knows I'm scared to death of frogs. (I don't know why—just am.) "That's the worst story ever. And besides, there aren't any frogs because the swamp creatures arose from the depths of the lake and took…." I stand up, looming over Mom and *BOOM!* lightening blasts through the window, and I crash back onto the bed.

"Now that was a little scary," Mom admits.

"Stormy nights. That's how every horror movie begins," I say, not kidding at all.

"Really?"

I start to explain, then realize she's baiting me. "At least the few I've seen. I don't even like horror movies, and I deplore tragic ones. I'm all about the triumph."

"I know you are," says Mom laughing, "and I love you very much."

"You too." I give Mom a hug and head to my palace.

As soon as I'm a star and have lots of money, I'm going to buy Mom everything she's ever wanted. She says she already has everything she wants. *Whatever.* I'm also going to have an enormous house for all the lonely people in the world to live in. Then there's my list of organizations…

I lie down on the pink canopy bed and pull the silky sheets over me. They feel so good and… *I'm so tired.* Today has been a major EMD (code for a "way too emotional day"). I lean over and take my diary out of my purse.

I feel my writing drift down the page as my eyes close. *My show is tomorrow.*

*** 3 ***

"After the chorus," I tell Brendon for the tenth time in five minutes.

"But I'm ready to rap now."

"When I squeeze your hand," I say calmly. Brendon and I peek through the curtain as the music begins...

"Time for a change
Things can't stay the same
Your way-my way-has gotten insane
If we work together, we can make it better
Things can't stay the same
Time for a change..."

"Now," I whisper. Brendon takes the mic and raps his way to the stage —

> *"We can make a difference-you and me*
> *If we embrace who we are, we'll find harmony*
> *This world's gone crazy-upside down*
> *It's up to me and you*
> *To turn it back around..."*

I wake up in the middle of Act 2. I really do know these songs in my sleep! I don't remember learning how to sing or write. But I remember wanting to get the songs in my head onto paper, like the ones in Mom's piano book. Mom framed the first one I wrote. It's a few color crayoned lines, but it rhymes.

Adults *oohed* and *aahed* when I sang and told me I belonged in Hollywood. However, when I got older and told everyone I was moving to Hollywood (or possibly New York City), as soon as possible, they just laughed and said, "How cute." Then they'd look at my parents like, "I don't envy you." And people love telling me how horrible the entertainment industry is (though I'm not exactly sure how they know this, since none of them are in it). Then there's the, "She's so talented," that sounds more like a curse than a compliment.

I'll never forget hearing Dad tell someone that he hoped I'd grow out of my "big dreams." It hurt so much I swear my heart stopped beating. My insides were enraged, and at the same time I wanted to crawl under the bed and hide. I finally told him I wasn't growing out of anything. Then I asked why he'd want me to grow out of being me. Instead of answering my question, he grounded me for being "disrespectful." Worse than feeling lonely sometimes (which I would never admit), is not having people who love you, or anyone for that matter, understand your dreams.

Mom doesn't completely understand, but she believes in me. Thank goodness for her and Brianna. Brianna and I are the same and different all at once. Same, as in she's as dedicated to her future profession as I am. Different, as in she's going to be a doctor—maybe even a surgeon. She'll probably cure cancer one day. Seriously, she's a major brain.

"Is anyone home?" shouts someone from outside.

The mail's here. "Don't go anywhere!" *I should have slept by the door.* I throw on my slightly wet, used to be beautiful outfit, and book it down the stairs, "I'm coming!" Mom's standing at the door. "Did you get it?" I ask out of breath.

"It's not the mail."

"Then who is it?"

"I'm not exactly sure. But they're here for you." Mom rubs her eyes. "I'm going back upstairs."

Tentatively, I walk outside. *Holy cow.* There are a dozen kids standing in the yard. And they're looking at me like I'm an alien. I check myself out in the window and gasp. My skirt turned into a short, crinkly mini skirt. The fur on my sweater looks like wet chicken feathers, and since I went to bed with wet hair—I have long, blonde, tangled dreadlocks.

"Hey, I'm Traci," says a girl running up the drive.

It's the girl from the bus…the one that pointed out the "bathroom." What…?

"Jesse dropped his breakfast," she says, explaining the dirty banana in her hand. "I'm babysitting and I didn't want to litter."

"You're not my babysitter!"

I guess that was Jesse. "I'm Kristi Kate."

Traci flashes a bright smile. "Cool."

"Why are all of you here? Not that I mind. I was just wondering."

"Are you kidding? You're the talk of the town! Well, if you can call this a town."

I could definitely elaborate on that statement. Instead, I nod in agreement. "How did you know where we were staying?"

"Obviously, you don't live in a small town," Traci answers.

I thought I did.

"No one ever comes here," Traci continues. "Especially to this house."

"We didn't plan on coming, see…" I stop myself

mid-sentence. Millions of thoughts (none of them good) are racing through my mind. "What do you mean? A friend of my dad's grandma lives here."

Traci's looking at me like I'm dead wrong. She even looks scared for me. "No one's been anywhere near this house ever since… I don't know if I'm allowed to talk about it."

I knew it. "MOM! MOM!"

"What's wrong?" Mom shrieks, running out of the house.

When she sees I'm not bleeding or being attacked by a bear or something, she gives me a look. (I don't think she appreciated my terror stricken shout.) Under normal circumstances, I'm not a screamer. But, hello! If there is anything we've learned in the last twenty-four hours, it's that looks are deceiving. Obviously, we're in danger. But I don't get to explain this, because the previously silent kids start babbling away and introducing themselves.

Traci looks amused. I have no idea what I look like. Mom is just smiling and saying hello like this is

NORMAL. She's acting so normal that it's freaking me out. (I have brought some semi-strangers home a few times, but this is entirely different.)

"Mom, these aren't my friends." *Ooh...that didn't sound good.* "I mean, you're not my friends yet. And Traci," I say, grabbing her hand and pulling her over so fast she loses her balance and almost falls down, "she's definitely my friend. She's the one who saved my life yesterday." Mom's lost. "By pointing out the bathroom, remember?"

Mom kind of nods. "Thank you, Traci."

"Oh, you're welcome," Traci smiles.

Mom looks at me. "But what is everyone doing here?"

Now I'm getting exasperated. One, because I forgot the whole reason I screamed in the first place. And two, Mom needs to get on board—we have to get out of here! "Mom." I pull her to the side. "This is not Dad's friend's grandma's house."

"What?"

"What if it's some kind of trap? What if..."

"Oh, please," Mom says, cutting me off. "I'm sure there is a logical explanation for this. But why are they here?"

"Traci said it's because the town's so small that no one ever comes here. It's like we're celebrities. And they came to warn us about the house."

Mom doesn't comment on the house part. She doesn't seem concerned at all. What she says is, "Well, you should like that."

"Like what?"

"The fact that we're like celebrities here."

Wow. With everything else going on, I didn't take that in.

"Now that I know you're alive and well, I'm going inside to see what I can find for breakfast."

How Mom's remaining so calm right now, is just beyond me. Doesn't she wonder why there's food in a house that no one has been in for years? Traci and the others have to be right. They're the ones who live here.

As for me—I need to rise up to the occasion.

They hiked all the way up to this house, and put their lives in danger just to meet me. The least I can do is sign some autographs. *I finally have the opportunity to practice being a star!* I smooth down my feathers, have a quick "get it together" talk with myself and… "I'm back!" Even though I didn't really go anywhere, I give a huge wave, like I've missed them my entire life. (Because that's what stars do.)

This is so much fun, I almost forget it's not for real. That is, until Traci tells me how psyched she is that I'll be here for the weekend. "I'm sorry, but I'm not going to be here for the weekend. It was great meeting all of you, but we're leaving in a few minutes."

Traci looks at me very seriously. This is not the same look she had when she told me about the house. "How? It's a holiday weekend."

If I didn't know she was joking, I'd pass out while standing up. But there's no holiday today; I love holidays. If this were a holiday, I would definitely know it. For some reason, my stomach tightens anyway. It's like my body is subconsciously warning me that something terrible is about to happen. *Please, Traci. Please, please, please tell me you're joking. Break out into outrageous laughter. Or something. Or anything.*

"It's not a national holiday or anything," continues Traci. "Everyone acts like it is—I think it's dumb, but…"

"But what?" I ask, afraid to breathe.

Words tumble out of Traci's mouth… "It's a holiday for our town that someone came up with years ago. There's a parade and all sorts of activities, and well, everything is closed. Everything—including the airport."

WHAT??!!!" Kids wince and Jesse covers his ears as my terror echoes through the trees. I don't care if I'm grounded for the rest of my life, as long as we're home in time for my show tonight. Mom doesn't meet me at the door to tell me I'm in trouble. *Not a good sign.* When I find her she has tears in her eyes. I know without asking. It's true.

"I am so, so sorry…" whispers Mom.

I hate that Mom's crying. I... wait. She knew about this? And she kept it from me? This upsets me more than anything—and that's A LOT of upsetness.

"I've only known for a few minutes," Mom says, reading my heart. "You were having so much fun outside…"

"Who cares about fun? My show is tonight! My show that's going to… The show I've been working on for…"

"Honey, I…"

"Tristian can come and get me. People drive with permits all the time!"

"I know how important this is to you, but…"

"No, you don't! No one does," I cry. What about Luke's mom?"

"We are not asking someone to drive eight hours to…"

"Then let's rent a car! I'll pay for it with my own money."

"There aren't…"

"What kind of stupid town is this? They don't

have taxis or rental cars, but they have some stupid airport that's closed for some stupid holiday?!"

"Maybe their holiday is as important to them as your show is to you."

Really? Like a zombie, I walk out the door.

Through a blurry world of green weeds, I notice everyone's gone. *So much for my star status.* Even Traci's gone. This makes me sadder. And it makes no sense. She's only been my friend for… not even a day. Still, it does.

Before long, I'm running. The weeds slap my bare legs. I don't know where I'm going, but the faster I run, the easier it is to breathe. *I wish I could jump into that lake.* Where is the dumb thing anyway? Everything looks the same—like a big mess.

I pause to catch my breath and swallow snot. Grosssssss. An eerie feeling comes over me. *I'm not alone.* And then I hear it—the crunchy sound leaves make when someone steps on them. I take off running and… *I should have never left when I could see how upset Mom was… It's not her fault…*

I shouldn't have... Now I'm... The footsteps are getting closer. I've got to hide. I stop abruptly and...

Wham! The chaser slams into me and I fall to the ground.

"Are you hurt? I just wanted..."

Traci? "Traci?" I cough.

"Yeah."

"Uuh...you're squashing me."

"Oh, sorry!" Traci jumps up. "So glad... I caught up with you. You're fast," she says, panting. "I hope I didn't freak you out. It's the exact opposite of what I wanted to do. But when I saw you yesterday, in that beautiful pink outfit, looking for a bathroom in the middle of nowhere, I knew... I just knew it."

I'm so confused. "What did you know?"

"I knew I had to meet you. I was coming over to introduce myself, but I got intimidated..."

"Of what?" I ask, dizzily.

"Anyway," Traci continues without answering me. "I had this great idea of bringing the neighbors with me—kind of like a welcome party for you," she says positively. "They were all into it, but then they got bored—that's where the haunted house story came in. I made it up to keep them entertained. I don't know anything about that house other than the lawn needs mowing. Though I did see a beautiful woman there one time. She looked magical, even from afar. Which is another reason I just had to meet you."

Traci shoots me a worried smile and continues pacing. "I didn't want your business all over town—and we could hear everything. So I mentioned that the lines were probably getting long at the fair and everyone bolted. Then I went down to the creek and counted to one hundred about a million times, waiting patiently for things to settle down. But when I went back, you were gone. Your mom said you had taken a walk. That you do that when you're upset. She said I was welcome to wait, but I couldn't wait any longer. And I definitely couldn't do the counting thing anymore—it was making me more impatient than usual. The ground was still wet from the rain last night so I followed your footprints. Then I heard you crying, so I ran faster. I'm sorry I scared you, and I'm really sorry I got you in trouble over nothing, and I'm terribly sorry that I knocked you down!"

I think she's done. Or maybe she's just stopping for air.

"Are you gonna say anything?" Traci asks.

I'm still on the ground, waiting for the world to stop spinning. I'm not sure if it's because she hit me in the head when she collided into me, the relief that it was her chasing me and not some madman, or the fact that I have never, in my entire life, heard anyone talk so fast.

Traci leans down and peers into my eyes. "Can you see my fingers?" she asks, waving her hand in front of my face. For some reason, I start laughing. I laugh so hard, that for a second, the last twenty four hours is just a bad dramedy that somehow—unwillingly, I have the leading role in. "Oh, no, oh no, oh no," Traci cries. "I think you have a concussion. I read that people with concussions have strange behavior, and continuous laughter is one of the signs!"

The more Traci freaks out, the harder I laugh. I can't help it. Finally, I manage to say, "Did you read that when you were bored?" Traci tilts her head to the side, uncertain of how to respond. "It was a joke," I cough, still laughing.

"Oh." Traci says, relieved.

"Can you help me up?" I reach for Traci's hand. "As far as the house thing, normally I wouldn't have been scared. But mom and I were making up scary stories last night so stuff like that was already in my head."

"I see," Traci nods.

"And with everything else going on, I just panicked."

"Ohmygosh!" Traci cries—like she's just made a revolutionary discovery. "You're in the midst of a crisis, and I'm just rambling away." Traci takes a seat on a stump and gives me her full attention. "Other than this place being the pits, what else is making you wanna be back where you live so much?"

Traci barely breathes as I walk her through the details of my dilemma. She does wave her hands like this is the worst story ever kind of wave, collapses on the ground, and covers her head a few times, but she doesn't say a word. (Very impressive for someone who just talked solid for ten entire minutes.) "And that's why you're meeting me on the most devastating day of my entire existence," I conclude.

Traci jumps up and throws her hands on her hips. "I can't believe this! I only thought I was sorry before. Now I'm the sorriest in the world that you got stuck here."

I don't think she meant to scream, but because nothing is around us, it echoes like she said it at the top of her lungs. We laugh—and then I fall to the ground. This time, on purpose.

"What's wrong? I thought you were feeling a little better."

"I was, until I remembered another part of my tragedy that I somehow forgot in the midst of ALL THESE WEEDS." For a second, Traci thinks I mean the actual weeds, and then realizes I mean mess. "Not only am I missing my show tonight, I'm missing the first date of my life, with the most awesome guy in the world, whom I could possibly love."

Traci's flabbergasted. "This just gets worse and worse."

"I know."

Still in shock, Traci plops down beside me. "You get to date?!"

"Well… it's not *exactly* a date. His mom's picking me up and taking us to the movies. Luke made her promise not to say anything. And they have a huge car, so I'm looking at it like she's our chauffeur."

"That's for sure almost a real date."

I give Traci a thank-you-for-understanding nod.

"But wait. How are you going to go to the movies and be in your show at the same time?"

Maybe I do have a concussion. "That was such an unwarranted breakdown."

"So, no date?" Traci asks.

"Yes, date. But it's the day after tomorrow. I guess I just…"

Traci interjects, "I have a confession to make."

I raise my eyebrows like this actress I'm studying does. (It's kind of like saying "Yes, what might it be?" or "Continue.")

"I'm truly sorry you got stuck here. But I'm a little excited too. There's no one like you here."

I start to ask her how she knows this, since she doesn't really know me, but…

"I just know. I've been praying for a friend like you."

Huh? "What about everyone you drug to my non-haunted house?"

"We have fun, but we don't have that much in common. Sometimes when we hang, I feel lonelier than I do than when I'm by myself." Traci pauses. "I don't think I've ever said that out loud."

I feel my face growing warm. "We should probably head back. I don't want Mom going overboard with worry," I say, standing up. "What's that building down there?"

"Used to be our church."

"Used to be?"

"When Mr. and Mrs. Whitman left everything kind of fell apart."

"Were they like the Pastor people?"

Traci nods. "They were amazing. They communicated with everyone in their own language."

"How many languages are there here?" I ask, wondering where all the culture is.

"I don't mean foreign languages," Traci hastily adds.

"What do you mean, then?"

"Whether you're ten, twenty, ninety, rich, poor, in love with God, or mad at God, they have a way of talking that makes you want to listen."

I want to be like that. "They sound like some friends of my mom's. Where did they go?"

"I don't know. I was too busy thinking about

how much I'd miss them and didn't catch that part. Ever since they left, it's been a mess."

"How so?"

"The first pastor was B-O-R-I-N-G. The next one yelled."

"Like a passionate yell or a mean scream?"

"Like if you sat in the front row you might get spit on kind of yell. After that, there was a nice little lady. She tried hard, but most people had already stopped coming."

"I probably would have too," I admit.

"Mom says people are always looking for a reason not to go to church, but instead of complaining and making excuses, we should be a part of the solution."

"Your mom sounds smart."

"She is. And I really miss church. It's the one thing that brought people together. Regardless of our differences, we had God in common. And I really miss choir," Traci says, now lost in her loss. "The only thing I liked about this holiday weekend was the…" Traci sees my face and stops.

"It's okay," I moan.

"Sorry!"

I shrug my shoulders. *I can take it.*

"The church always had something special on Sunday." Traci pauses. "Do you go? To church," she clarifies, when I don't answer.

"Not anymore."

"Why not?" Traci asks.

In my head, I hear myself asking Dad the same question. He said there were reasons. But he never said what the reasons were. "I can't remember. Mom and I pray every night though, and I'm always talking to God." *I wonder why we don't go anymore.*

"God's my best friend," says Traci. "Not that you can't be too! It's just different. You know."

I smile, wishing I knew exactly what she was talking about. "So the building just sits there, doing nothing?

"Pretty much."

"We should go check it out."

"Why?" asks Traci.

"I don't know. A deserted church, small town..."

"I thought you needed to get back," Traci laughs.

"I do, but…" *I'm not ready.*

"I'm sure it's locked," Traci says, in an I-don't-think-it's-a-very-good-idea-anyway voice.

"Maybe not, it's a church."

"Wouldn't that be like breaking and entering or trespassing?" Traci asks.

"No," I answer confidently. "If the door's open, it can't be breaking and entering." *Can it?* "If anyone questions why we're there, I'll say I needed to ask God what to do with my dilemma."

"Didn't you just say that you talked to God all the time?"

"Yeah. But officially, it is God's house. They don't know I personally feel God can hear me just as well right here. Especially when everything we say echoes ten times," I add.

"It does make sense," Traci says. "But since it's not true for you, doesn't that kind of make it a lie?"

I hadn't thought of it like that. I definitely don't

want to lie in God's house. Now I'm contradicting myself. I guess if God hears me no matter where I am, a lie—or a not so much the truth borderline lie, is just as bad "in the world" as it is in church. "You're right," I say, still wanting to go. I want to go more now than I did in the first place. "Let's first, hope no one comes in. If they do, we go for the truth; I desperately need prayer—so here we are."

Traci considers. "C'mon. Let's go."

*** 4 ***

After going through a lot of weeds, we stumble upon a perfectly clear path. "I've taken a million different routes to church," Traci says, bewildered. "But I've never seen this path."

"I told you. We're meant to explore it." As soon as the words are out of my mouth, we come upon a wide, murky creek that's directly in our way.

Traci gives me a or-maybe-we're-not look. "I guess we can walk through it."

Whew. For a second, I thought our adventure was over. "I don't care about my clothes." *At least not anymore.* "But I'm concerned about our feet."

"Our feet?" questions Traci.

"We went to Six Flags last year. Everyone told me not to ride the water ride first, but I was sticky hot, so I did it anyway. It was like my body was drinking an ice cold glass of water. But then I had to squish around in my soaked shoes all day. I could feel my toes getting punier by the second. It was one of those things where the more you try to ignore it, the more you think about how gross it feels. Put it like this, it was an un-fun day."

"We could ditch our shoes, offers Traci.

"Yeah, but who knows what's on the bottom. There could be glass, or even worse—that slippery, slimy stuff." I can hear Brianna's voice in my head. *If you have a tiny cut, even one so small you don't even know it's there, you're exposing it to bacteria—which could result in traumatic infections that could possibly be fatal.* Actually, Brianna would have said it much better. She's so medically minded that I don't always understand what she's saying. But I get the bottom line—don't do it. "I'm going to leap over it."

Traci speculates. "I'll climb over on that log."

I can see myself falling off that log, so I prepare for my leap. "One, two, three..." *Still here.* I need a running start. "One, two, three..." My left foot lands in a pile of mud. But most of me made it! I grab a branch and pull the rest of me out.

Traci inches herself across the log, while I beat the mud off one shoe and rub the other one in the grass to get it dry. "Your way was faster," Traci says, finally making it over.

"Yours was cleaner."

After a few more minutes, the church looms before us. It looks different up close. *Intimidating.* (It's not going to stop me from exploring—I'm just stating it for the record.)

"Let's say a prayer before we go in," Traci suggests.

I look down at myself. "I think we should have said one before we crossed the creek."

"Dear Lord," Traci begins. "Thank You for letting us reach our destination safely."

Without meaning to, I laugh. "I am thankful,"

I apologize. "It was just funny how you said it." We hesitate for a second, then I reach for the door. *Darn!* It's locked.

"There's a side door," Traci remembers. We run to the side and... the side door is wide open! A rush of adrenaline shoots through my body. "Why's the door open?" Traci wonders out loud.

"A definite sign we're supposed to be here," I proclaim. Traci's skeptical, but walks in anyway. The first thing we notice is the silence. Normally, silence is silence. But you can actually *hear* this silence. "Where are the lights?"

Traci flips some switches. "Right here, I think."

It takes a second for our eyes to adjust, and when they do, it's as if someone deserted their own dinner party. Dirty plates and empty cups are everywhere. "You'd think a church would be cleaner than anything. Except maybe a hospital."

Traci agrees. "Let's clean up."

"Do you think it will counteract our sneaking in?" I ask, knowing that's what she's thinking.

"Maybe," she smiles.

After throwing the last plate in the garbage, Traci leads me into the main room. Sunshine pours in through the stained glass windows, and there's a stage... with microphones... and a piano... "Hey, weren't you singing yesterday?"

"I'm always singing." Traci looks away. "When I sing..."

"You feel the opposite of lonely. Like everything is right in the world and anything is possible," I say softly.

"How do you..."

"Why didn't you say something when I was talking about the show?" I ask, not wanting to answer the question I knew she was going to ask. "Sing something!"

"You're the guest. You go first."

In the back of my mind, the clock is ticking—I need to get back, so I can deal with not getting back. "You think it's okay?"

"Considering I don't know if it's okay to be here, I'm sure it's fine."

"I'm so glad I met you," I laugh, running over to the piano. I run my fingers over the chords, and bye-bye silence. It sounds like I'm in a major recording studio. (Not that I've been in one yet—but still.) "This one is called *It's My Time*." I'm lost in the music before I even begin.

> *"All this time*
> *Been fighting the lies*
> *No one could understand*
> *Laughing at my dreams*
>
> *But here I am*
> *Not gonna hide*
> *Heart's open wide*
> *It's my time*
>
> *It's my time*
> *It's my time to shine*
> *All I got inside*
> *Is coming alive, it's coming alive*
> *It's my time*

Chance is here
Good-bye fear
Want the world to see
What's inside of me

It's my time
It's my time to shine..."

On the second time through, Traci joins me on the chorus. We end with a bang and a bow applauding ourselves. "That was awesome!"

"I've never had so much in my life," Traci exclaims.

"Well, don't stop now," I say, urging her on.

Traci takes a breath and begins. She sings acappella and sounds like an angel. I'm trying to figure out the harmony when… *Footsteps.* I hear footsteps. *No way!* My new found joy flips to fear, and I turn to Traci. "Come on," she whispers, answering the question I didn't ask.

We duck behind an ancient looking organ that I hope doesn't collapse on our heads.

Legally, I don't think we're doing anything wrong.

What I didn't think about was the fact that this place is perfect for escaped convicts. You could hide in the weeds for days, drink water from the creek, and no one would suspect a criminal to be in a church. Temporary shelter, leftover food, coins lying around from the offering... I glance at Traci—she's praying. I close my eyes to do the same, but my mind is wild with what-ifs.

"I'm not crazy." *A woman's voice.*

Traci's eyes pop open and she leans forward.

"Someone was singing. And I know that voice," says the woman.

"See, no one is down here," says a man.

"You're right," she sighs. "There's no reason she'd be in an empty church on a Saturday," she says, trying to laugh at herself. "I just wish..."

Their voices drift down the hall, but just when I think it's safe to breathe—Traci leaps to her feet!

"Mr. and Mrs. Whitman?"

"Oh my goodness! See Tom, I was right."

I thought those voices sounded familiar, but with

everything else going on, I thought I was crazy. "Mr. Tom? Mrs. Trish?" Their eyes light up like Christmas trees.

"How do you know?" Traci asks, dumbfounded.

"How do you?" I interrupt.

"This is Mr. and Mrs. Whitman! The ones who used to run the church."

"Remember how I said they sounded like friends of my mom's? This is them! I guess I never knew their last names." *Unbelievable.*

Traci and I are so busy talking over each other (yet fully understanding each other), that for a minute, we totally forget about Mr. and Mrs. Tom and Trish Whitman. "Don't you want to know how we know each other?" I ask, surprised they haven't already asked us.

"Yeah," chimes Traci. "Don't you wanna know?"

They exchange a look. It's a look you have with someone you've loved for a zillion years. A look only the two of you understand. *I want to have that with someone one day.*

"We're most interested," they say in unison. "But we're not surprised." *We can barely believe all this ourselves, and they're not even surprised?* "I have a feeling God put you two together on purpose," says Mrs. Whitman. *Traci said she was praying for a friend like me. What does…?*

Mr. Whitman clears his throat, "But do tell us, how you, Miss Kristi Kate, happen to be in Alabama, and how you met our Traci?"

"Or dear, maybe Traci met her first."

Traci and I hold our giggles (they're the cutest), and begin…

"And there you go," says Traci, matter-of-factly.

"Can you believe it?" I ask, blown away by our own stories.

Mrs. Whitman puts her hand on my shoulder. "I imagine those songs have wanted to burst out of your heart since before time began. And to see the children you taught perform."

"And the teachers, even some of your peers I'm guessing, getting to see how talented and dedicated you are. I've seen too much in my life to call it a tragedy exactly, but my, what a disappointment," says Mr. Whitman.

I'm glad they get what a landmark event this was going to be, but they're making me feel even worse.

"And poor Traci..." sighs Mrs. Whitman.

Mr. Whitman politely interjects. "Now not having a real church could seriously become a tragedy. When people don't know there's a purpose and a plan for their life..." He shakes his head. "It leads to a lot of bad decisions."

"And without knowing who they are in Christ, and how much God loves them...Well, we try to fill those voids in our heart and mind with anything that makes us feel important. Better for the moment," adds Mrs. Whitman.

They look at each other and nod. This look, I know. It means drugs, teen sex, cheap thrills, gangs... things that lead to life (not just grounded) trouble. *Things my dad thinks only exist in Hollywood.*

"Now Traci, you were always talking about getting

a music scholarship. How is this going to happen if you don't have a place to practice?" Mr. Whitman asks.

"I practice in the shower," Traci says, ready to cry.

This is completely incomprehensible! What has happened to the uplifting, encouraging Whitmans?

"I'm sure it took quite of bit of persuading for the school board to allow your show to happen at all, Kristi Kate. What happens now?" Mr. Whitman interrogates.

"I'm going to find a place outside of school, where we can have an additional performance." *I am?* "That way I won't have to have the school's permission. All I'll need is the parent's." *This is brill!!!*

"Now that's a good idea," says Mrs. Whitman.

Finally! Something positive.

"Teachers might see it as disrespectful," Mr. Whitman interjects. "Going above them and taking matters into her own hands and all."

"Maybe not, Tom."

Oh, yes they will! And the last thing I need is more

complications at school. It's bad enough I have to go in general.

"The permits might be an issue though," Mrs. Whitman continues.

Permits? "What kind of permits?" They start explaining—I get dizzier. "I'm sure I'll figure everything out," I respond with my fake confidence.

"We're sure you will," Mrs. Whitman says.

After a few more minutes, we say our goodbyes, and watch them walk away. "Are they acting strange or it is us?" I mouth to Traci.

"We have an idea!" Mrs. Whitman says, bursting back in.

"It's more than an idea, states Mr. Whitman. "It's a God idea. This town needs a real church and Traci, you need a place to sing. Kristi Kate, you were born to create and perform..."

We have no idea where they're going with this, but it's sure making us feel better than all the other stuff they were saying.

"What Tom is saying..." Mrs. Whitman clears

her throat. "Traci, use your leadership skills in a positive way and get everyone in this town together."

Traci looks at me—I'm clueless. "What am I getting them together for?"

"To perform in a show that you and Kristi Kate will put together for the church's annual holiday performance," she says easily.

"What?!?" Traci and I both exclaim at the same time, "Are you talking about?"

"Isn't the show usually on Sunday?" asks Mrs. Whitman.

"Yeah," says Traci, still in shock at their suggestion.

"Well, then that's perfect," the Whitmans conclude.

"I can't get…"

"Didn't you just talk half the town into accompanying you to a somewhat deserted house, with a made up story, just so you could meet Kristi Kate?" asks Mrs. Whitman.

"Yes, Ma'am."

"Then why on earth couldn't you talk them into participating in a show?" she asks, sincerely serious.

"Some could sing, some could dance, some could make signs, others could spread the word around town…"

"Even if I could do that, we don't have a show for them to perform in."

Mrs. Whitman turns to me. "Didn't you just say you created and directed an entire show that's being performed tonight?"

"Yes, Ma'am," I stutter. "But we worked on that for months. There's no way…"

"I guess you're right, though it did sound like a God idea," Mrs. Whitman sighs. "Sometimes we live so strongly in our disappointments, that we don't see the amazing possibilities right in front of us. Sometimes, they're the greatest ones thus far, but we're so busy looking behind, we miss out."

All of a sudden, my brain feels like a car that's zoomed into the full speed ahead mode. "We could do a mini-version of the show. The catchy songs that are easy to learn. Traci knows who's good at what, so we won't need to have auditions. This will save tons of time and avoid a million arguments." I glance at Traci—she looks like I might have lost my mind. She might be right, but I don't have time to think about it right now, because there is NO WAY I'm going to look at the closed door anymore, when this one is being thrown wide open! "It could be the beginning of a brand new, cool, fun church. We can have a sign-up sheet for anyone who wants to teach a class, and… Traci? Say something."

"We should charge admission. Start a fund for the church," says Traci, coming out of her comatose shock state. "We'll invite everyone!"

"Are you sure?" I exclaim.

"Yes! For every reason Mr. and Mrs. Whitman said, and for every reason we don't even know of yet."

Mr. Whitman throws his hands in the air. Mrs. Whitman pretends to jump up and down with Traci and me. And right in the middle of cheering it hits me—Mom has no idea where I am right now.

★★★ 5 ★★★

Traci's mom runs out of the house when she sees Mr. and Mrs. Whitman. I try not to squirm while they reminisce. I realize that if it weren't for them, none of this would be happening, but I've got to get back and explain to Mom where I've been, so it can happen! (In my defense, I really had no idea where I was going. At my imagination's best, I couldn't have dreamed this up.) Traci gets this—

"This is my Mom, Jackie. Mom, this is Kristi Kate. She's the creator and director of the show you'll have the privilege of seeing tomorrow. I'll be starring in it as well." Jackie's eyebrows go up like *you two are very ambitious.* "Don't worry, we're not doing it by ourselves. We're gonna get the whole the town involved."

"By tomorrow night?" Jackie asks.

"You always say, with God all things are possible," quotes Traci.

Traci's mom smiles. "I do say that."

"And then you tell me to get to work."

Jackie nods. "See ya later."

"Thank you!" we both exclaim.

"Can Kristi Kate spend the night? Or, if it's alright with her parents, can I spend the night with her?"

"Don't you think you'll get more sleep before your big day if you're in your own house?"

"We probably won't even have time to sleep. And if we do, at least if we're together and one of us has a brilliant idea, we can just wake the other one up to work on it."

"Or maybe we'll take turns sleeping so one of us can always be working," I add.

"Exactly. And besides, it's not Kristi Kate's real

house anyway, so she'll sleep the same no matter what." Traci's mom agrees and says to call her later.

I hope my mom agrees. And I hope when she sees me with the Whitmans, it will get me out of any trouble I might be in. On second thought, that would really put Mom on the spot. When Mom has something serious to talk to me about, she always waits until we're by ourselves. I should give her the same respect. Not that she's in trouble. It just seems like the same kind of thing. "I'll be right back," I say, as we pull into the driveway.

To my surprise, Mom is sitting outside on the steps reading. She doesn't *look* upset. But as soon as she hears me, she looks up expectantly. "I hope you weren't worried," I say, sitting down beside her.

"I'm always worried." Mom points to her book, 'Worry about nothing, Pray about everything.' "I don't know if I'll ever have it mastered, but I got some good practice in today."

"I'm sorry I ran off. And I'm sorry... I know none of this is your fault."

"It's not, but I'm sorry too." I lean my head into Mom's shoulder. Part of me wants to stay like this forever.

After a second, Mom tells me how she trusts me, but part of that trust is based on my keeping her in the loop. In other words, this was an unusual day and we're okay, but if I pull something like this again, we won't be. I assure her that I won't. (I know kids who hide things from their parents. I also know parents who snoop through their kid's stuff. I never want that kind of relationship with anyone. Especially my mom.)

"Oh, your new friend was looking for you earlier. A lot earlier. Where have you been, anyway? I see lots of dirt, muddy shoes, some sparkles in your pretty blue eyes…"

"Close *your* pretty blue eyes. I'll be right back."

"Now I'm worried," Mom sighs.

I run down the driveway—this time, coming back with Traci and the Whitmans. "Surprise!"

"How in the world?" Mom cries. We quickly

share our wonderfully crazy morning with her. "This is amazing," Moms says, hugging the Whitmans. And to Traci and me, "I want a front row seat, for what I know is going to be a ground-breaking, show-stopping event." I love that Mom skips right over the *what?!?* page.

All of a sudden, my stomach lets out a major growl. "Hungry?" Traci laughs.

"Starving, I guess. What time did you come over this morning?"

"Umm, around seven."

"Oh, yeah. If you can get people up that early on a Saturday—we're good to go. Speaking of time, I need to make some calls. You can wait…"

"I'll ask the Whitmans to drop me off. You can meet me when you're done."

"You don't mind?"

Traci shakes her head. "We should switch clothes."

Is she crazy? Why would she want…

"Since you weren't planning on being here, I'm guessing you don't have any other clothes with you.

You can put on mine, and I'll wear yours home. My mom sews. She's good. Maybe she can…

I look in the mirror. I'm what Brianna calls a MM (code for a Major Mess). "She's going to have to be a miracle worker."

Before Traci leaves, I ask Mom if she can spend the night. "It's fine with me, but I'll have to call Joe before I can say yes."

"I'm sure it will be fine. If the grandma is the type of person who lets her grandson's friends stay here, what's one more friend of a friend?"

"You're probably right, but it'd be easier if you just stayed with Traci."

"True. But none of this is exactly easy. And Traci always stays at her house. If she stays here, we're both somewhere new. It will help us prepare for our new show and new day tomorrow."

Mom never rolls her eyes, but she has a look that's equivalent to it. "I'll give Joe a call. But first…"

"I need to call Jasmyn, and Brendon and Tabitha…"

"And Ms. Smith."

"And Ms. Smith," I sigh.

"Would you like me to talk to her?"

Yes, I absolutely would. "I need to do this myself." Mom nods like she was hoping I'd say that. I take her phone and instinctively go to the grandma's—I mean Delilah's room. There's wisdom in here. And so many experiences. As I dial Ms. Smith's number, something tells me mine are just beginning. Ms. Smith answers on the first ring (of course). I try to sound as calm as possible, but what I had planned to say, sounded much better in my head. Least my voice wasn't shaking. I finish explaining and hold my breath.

"You've worked so hard. I know you're disappointed. Is there anything I can do?"

I'm so relieved that I almost start to cry. *Almost.* Instead, "Thank you so much. And yes, please tell everyone how sorry I am. And would you mind hanging out back stage? We've rehearsed so much, I'm sure everything will be fine, but…"

"I'll be glad to." Ms. Smith is so positive, that

without planning on it, I tell her my idea of an additional performance. "That's an interesting idea," she says. "But let's talk about it when you return. Today's events seem like enough for today." She doesn't know the half of it.

I make myself call Jasmyn next. My heart hurts for her. It's going to be one more time someone lets her down. And this time, it's me.

"What's wrong?" Jasmyn asks, as soon as she hears my voice.

I briefly fill her in—and listen to her silence. Jasmyn's disappointment has to do with way more than the play. *And with each disappointment we lose a little piece of our heart. It gets harder and harder to believe.* Almost on automatic, I push this knowingness aside. I don't have time to go there today. Besides, this is about Jasmyn.

In the middle of explaining, I stop. "Forget the reasons. It stinks. You deserve everyone who promises you something to follow through. We all deserve that. I shouldn't have gone on what was supposed to be a day trip. I should have thought about all the what-ifs." I pause for a second. "Can I share something with you?" I feel Jasmyn nodding, pushing her hair back from her sweet face. *I wonder if I'm doing the right thing, she's only nine.* My gut says to go for it. "When I begged the teachers to let me do this, it was for me. I wanted to prove that I'm more than "just a dreamer." I wanted the girls who make fun of me to…"

"Girls make fun of you?" Jasmyn asks, finally speaking. "Why? You're so pretty, almost like a movie star. Wait, I shouldn't have said that." *Why? That's awesome!* "You're way more than pretty. You make everyone feel special. You like us the way we are," Jasmyn says softly. "Why do they make fun of you?"

I wish I knew. "I used to drive myself crazy wondering the same thing. I got brave and asked once. Most of them gave me a weird look and kept on going wherever they were going. However, there were a few who happily and loudly told me that they hated the way I looked, the way I dressed, and that I was a snob." (Which is odd, since they're the ones who won't speak to me.)

"That's dumb," whispers Jasmyn.

"Yeah. But it still hurts."

"Yeah."

"My mom says sometimes people are scared of anyone who isn't just like them. Anyway, I started out doing the show for myself, but somewhere along the way it changed."

"What happened?" asks Jasmyn.

"All of you were having fun with kids you normally don't even talk to." *Life was more like I want it to be.* "That seemed like a much better reason than my initial one."

"Thanks for trusting me."

"Thanks for being you."

"Huh?"

"Thanks for being you, Jasmyn."

"No one's ever said that to me before."

"Well, today is a new day, and now someone has.

So. Is anyone going to get to hear your sensational voice tonight?"

"Do you think if I sing loud enough, you'll be able to hear me in that weird place you're in?"

"Maybe!" I laugh.

Jasmyn tells me she needs to get off the phone and get ready—she knows I'm counting on her. *I'm hoping for her.* "Kristi Kate?" Jasmyn says before hanging up. "It wasn't wrong for you to go. If we let all the what-ifs stop us, we'd never do anything. And that'd be terrible. Right?"

"Right." The phone buzzing in my ear reminds me to hang up. *Wow.*

Tabatha doesn't want to come to the phone, but I hear her in the background, "I practiced all night. I can even say my lines backwards!"

As soon as Brendon hears the word airplane—it's all about the plane. When he finally gets the part that I'm not going to be there, he replies, "Don't worry about it. I really didn't want to be in the thing anyway. I'll go over to Jason's house and hang."

81

Panic. "Oh, no! Your part is very important, and you *really* need to be there." After a lot of convincing, he finally agrees.

"Okay, okay, if it means that much to you I'll do it. But who's going to tell me when it's time to rap?"

"Ms. Smith."

"Cool, I like her. Are you sure you can't come? Airplanes are really fast, you know."

I don't even try to explain this one. I just tell him to have fun and that I'll be there as fast as the airplane will fly me there—which won't be tonight. But "Yes, I'll bring you a picture of the airplane."

"How did it go?" Mom asks.

"Nerve racking and heart wrenching. But overall, I think it went as well as it could."

Mom gives me an understanding smile. "That's all you can hope for. And now, I think you have something else to do."

I do.

✶✶✶ 6 ✶✶✶

Traci opens the door before I even knock. "Sorry I'm late."

"Doesn't matter, come in. Mom had a great idea that just saved us hours. There's food on the table, help yourself to whatever," she says offhandedly. "Our future cast is at the carnival, so we went ahead and called their parents and asked if their child were interested, did they have their permission to participate."

Since my mouth is full, I raise my eyebrow. I guess I'm getting good at it because Traci gets that I have no idea why this is important.

"If they have to run home to ask their parents,

they might get bored in the process and never show up."

"Why can't they just call or text?"

"Before I tell you, you have to promise me you won't have a heart attack."

Technically, I don't think you can promise not to have a heart attack, but Traci's so serious that I go ahead and do it. "I solemnly swear not to have a heart attack."

"Excellent. First of all, the reception is horrid around here."

Inconvenient, yet not surprising. "Continue."

Traci's face tells me to brace myself. "Not everyone is allowed to text."

"What? Why? That's completely Un-American! Is it even legal?"

Traci moans. "I don't know who or what started it, but it came down to 'Texting is a superficial form of communication. If someone has something to say, they can pick up the phone.' Even some of the parents who usually aren't so old school ended up making a no-texting rule. So with that and bad reception, it leads to a lot of running around."

"It's possible I would have a heart attack if I couldn't text. I almost had one just because I forgot my charger." *I can't believe I'm getting ready to say this.* "But sometimes… I think the same thing."

"Oh, dear," says Traci, sensing my dilemma.

"At least you don't have to go to the gym for a workout." Traci looks at me like I've just said the dumbest thing. Then it hits me—there isn't a gym. I also realize that unwillingly, I'm making Traci feel worse about where she lives. *And to think, I've complained every day of my life about living in a small town.* "Who cares about texting and gyms? Gyms are just full of sweaty people running miles on a treadmill going nowhere. You actually go places when you run."

Traci gives me a thanks-for-trying smile. "I can text," she reassures me. "And I can deal with all the civilized things we're missing here. It's the LIFE I'm missing that makes me want to be anywhere but here. I'm not living my life, I'm reading about it.

And by the time the books get here, they're probably ten years old. Oh good gosh, I never even thought of that until now!"

This is bad. I have to think of something to cheer Traci up fast. "Maybe you can come live with me!"

Traci's face instantly lights up. "Do you think your parents would let me?"

I have no clue, but "Maybe. I used to ask for a sister all the time. I haven't mentioned it in a while, because if they had a baby now, I'd end up babysitting all the time. And that would be the death of my social life." *That I hope to have soon.* "But this would be perfect. I think there's a definite possibility they might say yes." Traci shrugs her shoulders in defeat—and defeat is not even in the picture yet. "Will your Mom not let you? Or do you not want to live with me?"

"Are you kidding? Living with you would be like living in an adventure all the time! It's my Mom. If she talked with your parents and they were really okay with it, she'd probably say yes."

"Then why do you look like you've been run over by a truck?"

"Because she'd say yes. She'd say it was a once in a lifetime opportunity and that I should go for it. She wants me to have more opportunities than she did. She's talked about moving, but we just don't have the money. And no matter how much I'd love to, I'd never leave my mom here by herself. Thanks for asking though. That in itself means a lot."

Wow. Okay... "Maybe your mom could come too! We have a huge house and my mom needs a fun friend."

"We would love that! But wait—wouldn't that be a little weird, all of us in your house? Even if your mom doesn't mind, your dad might not be into it."

She's right about this. But I'm way too excited to let go of this idea. *Where there's a will there's a way.* "Alright, I've got it."

"You do?" Traci asks, incredulously.

"I think so. Maybe my dad can stay here."

Traci looks at me like I've just grown ten heads. "Are you bonkers?"

"No. This could absolutely work. Amazingly enough, my dad loves small towns. He grew up in one. He's always saying how they have history, true character, a stronger ethic system, or something like that. He could work at—or maybe even buy, that so called airport. He could expand it. Really do something for the community. He'd end up being a hero and my dad LOVES recognition." *Note to self: this is the selling part of my plan.* "Eventually, your mom will have saved enough money for you to afford your own place. Then, due to all the renovations and upgrades he will have done, Dad can sell the airport at an astronomical price and come home."

"I should contact our local paper," I say, falling more in love with my idea every second. "They can write a story—better yet, they can start a column, a string of articles, about our getting stuck here, how Dad saw the town's need, and even though it was a huge sacrifice to be away from his family, he knew in the end everyone would benefit. Or some sort of blah, blah, blah stuff. He'll be a hero in both places. He's going to love this idea! I just have to figure out the best way to present it to him. Traci? Traci?"

"Please. Oh please," Traci pleads in a terror-stricken, barely audible voice.

"Please what?"

"Please tell me you're not planning on asking—or even mentioning this to your dad when you ask him about the show."

"Of course, I'm not." *I totally forgot about that.* I shove the thought to the back of my mind. (The reality of doing it is hours away, unlike this situation which is urgent.) "Well, in all honesty, I hadn't thought that far in advance. The plan just zapped into my brain five minutes ago. But you're right. It might not be the best time to present my brilliant idea to him."

"Might not be? MIGHT be the understatement of the century. I have an idea."

"Go," I say expectantly.

"How about you stick to one brilliant idea a day,"

Traci laughs. "You can store the others in a dream bank or something."

"Never! But I love the idea of a dream bank," I say impressed. "Great concept."

"I thought you two would be long gone," Traci's mom says, walking into the kitchen.

"We got a little side tracked." Traci grabs me, her purse, and the remains of our lunch. "Be back soon, love you."

"Thanks for lunch. By the way, how do you feel about roommates?" I don't get to hear her response, because Traci yanks me out the door. "Okay, okay, I get it. Back to now." *For now.* "So what do all the non-text parents have to say?"

Traci studies the list. "Timmy's mom said sure, as long as we can get him to say yes—doesn't sound that positive, but at least we have his mom's permission."

I try to say "uh huh" while chewing and almost choke. Listening, eating, carrying a bunch of stuff, and walking at a jogging pace is a little tricky.

"Robin's mom says she'll love it and wants to

know what she can do to help. Jesse's dad says that his son will be in the show whether he wants to or not. Geeze," sighs Traci. "Let's see… she left everyone else messages and asked them to call back on this number."

"Perfect," I say. *I wonder if we have to invite Jesse's dad.*

"Oh, there's more," Traci says, turning the sheet over. "Tyrell's mom said of course, and asked if the Whitmans would be there…"

"I wish they were going to be," I interrupt. "They never did tell us where they were going, just that they had to be *moving on*."

"Maybe they're on the way to tell someone else about their God idea."

"You think?!"

"Maybe," says Traci, going back to the list. "Courtney's mom said sure and…"

"What?" I ask.

"She wants to know what Courtney should wear,

if she needs to bring anything, how long we'll be rehearsing and a bunch of other stuff."

Traci's voice sounds like my stomach feels. "We're low on the details."

Traci peers into the distance. "Faith or Fear?"

"What?"

"Mom says when you're at a cross-road—when doubt pounces on your plans, that you have a choice. You have to pick a side."

I let this sink in. "Because you can't play on both sides." *Faith, confidence in what you hope for and assurance of what you can't see.* "I choose Faith."

★★★★★★★★★★

"Rachel, Timmy, Robin, come here!" yells Traci.

"Did they just see us and take off in the opposite direction?"

"Yeah," Traci replies, not believing it either. "What's going on?" Traci asks, when we finally catch up with them.

"Timmy said Kristi Kate was probably mad at us for getting her into trouble," answers Rachel.

"Cuz we could hear her screaming even when we were half way down the hill," Timmy adds.

"I'm not mad. I'm beyond glad you came over."

"You are?" Robin asks

"Oh, yeah, and I can't wait to tell you why. Do you know where everybody is?"

"Pretty much," answers Robin.

"Why don't the three of you go get everyone," Traci suggests. "And then we'll explain everything."

"Why can't you tell us now?" asks Timmy.

"Because we don't have time to explain it twenty seven times," I say, in my most patient voice. "Trust me—you will love it."

"But how can we get everybody to leave all the fun they're having, if we don't tell them what this thing they're gonna love so much is?" Robin asks practically.

"I'm sure you'll think of something," I say.

"But don't make up any stories like I did," Traci

interjects. "Just tell them the truth—that Kristi Kate and I say it's the coolest thing to ever happen in this town. And the faster they get here, the sooner they'll know what it is."

"Worst case scenario, if they don't want to be a part of it, they can go back to whatever they were doing," I add. "But if they don't come, they'll always wonder what they missed."

"I *know* I wanna be a part of whatever it is!" Rachel exclaims. "We'll be back in a minute," she says, grabbing Timmy and Robin.

I smile at Traci, "Nice. Can I borrow your phone?"

After getting disconnected at least three times (Traci wasn't kidding about the reception), Mom finally answers. "Guess who I talked to?"

"Who?"

"Delilah."

"Really?"

"She thinks it's *splendid* what you and Traci are doing, and…"

"She said splendid?" I interject.

"Splendid," Mom repeats. "And guess what else? She said she knows how much work you have ahead of you and suggested that Traci just spend the night."

"That sounds just like her," I respond in awe.

She also told me where the grocery is, so I'm going to walk over and pick up something for dinner."

Beep. Beep. "Mom, the phone's…"

"Love you," she says, as I toss the phone to Traci.

"This better be good," says a red-headed boy, coming up the hill.

"Hey, Todd," Traci says without looking up. Then to me, "We had six messages from parents giving their permission."

"Yes!" I whisper to Traci. Then I stand up and give everyone a big wave, "Thanks for coming."

"If you weren't on our outing this morning," Traci says, in a very official voice, "this is Kristi…"

"Yeah, we know," says Todd.

"Okay… so…we went to church this morning," Traci begins, "and Mr. and Mrs. Whitman, who are also friends of Kristi…"

"Mr. and Mrs. Whitman?"

"Why were you at church?"

"How does she know them?"

"What are they doing here?"

"Are they coming back?"

All these voices, asking all these questions and more. Traci and I look at each other—*what to do?* We silently sit down and cross our legs. As soon as they realize the only two people with answers are the only ones not talking, they chill. "I promise I'll answer all your questions… like Monday," says Traci. "But right now, time is of essence…"

Half-way through I take over. "So I'm telling the Whitmans my tragic story, and Traci's sharing how you don't have a real church anymore, and they had an idea…"

"A God idea," says Traci.

"Right," I say, thanking her. "They said we needed to put on a show for tomorrow night's festival."

"What?" cries our future cast. "Tomorrow? No way."

"That's what we thought too," says Traci.

"But when we said that out loud, Mrs. Whitman said the saddest people in the world are the ones full of excuses—the ones who live in regret of what might have been. She said when we focus on the past, we let the greatest breakthroughs and the most amazing opportunities fly right by, then *Boom*!" I say with emphasis. "Another door, slammed in our face."

"She said all that?" asks Tyrell. "She must have been seriously bummin."

In my head, that's exactly what she said, but...

"She didn't say it exactly like that, but it's definitely what she meant," says Traci, clearing my words up.

"And I'm not about to be one of those people," I say, taking a sip of water. "God's practically throwing this opportunity in our laps."

"Who's in?" asks Traci.

"I'm not singin or dancin," says Cameron.

"No problem. If you don't want to sing, we have a list of other things you can do," I say, excited.

"Right on," says Cameron. "But I gotta ask my mom."

"I almost forgot," says Traci. "My mom knows we're rushed on time, so she called your parents and asked IF you were interested, would it be okay. We have a list of everyone she spoke to and what they said."

"I was trying to conserve my energy, but hey, if I don't have to run another five miles to go get permission, I'll be in it," says someone.

While Traci's dealing with the permission issues, I tackle the few who don't seem interested. "Todd, right?"

"Yeah."

"You going to hang with us?"

"Sounds lame."

"Lame? As in boring? I would never, least by choice, do anything boring."

Todd looks at me like he might believe this, but doesn't really care. "Sounds lame to me."

I shrug my shoulders. "I guess everyone has their

own idea of what lame is." He seems surprised by my response. I am too, especially since I've never realized this before. "I would hate for you to be bored on your weekend off. Too bad though. We could use your help."

"You'll be fine."

"We will," I say confidently. "I just don't know how we're going to move the piano and the tables. They're heavy and you look strong." *I'm good at this!* "I was just hoping..."

Todd looks around, "I'm the strongest guy here, for sure."

"So, you think..."

"Sure," Todd says, in a well-practiced, I'm-doing-you-a-big-favor voice.

"You rock, Todd. Traci didn't have your number, but you can use her phone to call your parents."

"I don't need to. They'll let me."

We so need another day for this. "I'm sure they will. But my Mom said we have to get permission from every parent, or else no show."

"Dude. Your parents are strict."

I give a sad nod, "Yeah." He agrees to call and I'm on to the next one. Which is… Gretchen. (My dad doesn't understand how I can remember the name of every person I've ever met, and lyrics to every song I've ever heard, but can't remember simple fractions. The only logical explanation I can think of is that songs and people make me smile, and math gives me a massive headache.) Gretchen looks about seven and is very shy. So far, all I've gotten is some umms. There has to be something…

"I got to help out with a really cool music class last summer," I begin. There was this one girl, who I knew was going to be a great singer. Her voice sounded pretty even when she talked. But she did not want to sing. Well, one day I saw a picture she'd drawn of a little girl with a microphone. I asked her who the girl was and she said it used to be her. She told me she used to sing all the time, but that one day her brother and his friends spied on her and told her that she sounded like a frog. They went around the house ribbitting for days. The more upset she got, the louder they'd ribbit. It made her so upset, she decided she was never singing again."

"That's terrible," says Gretchen.

"I know," I sigh, so happy that she speaks. "Words can sting stronger than bees. But I told her that if she believes everything people say about her, that instead of saying *ribbit, ribbit*, they'll be saying, *crazy, crazy*. Because if we let everyone who says something silly or mean stop us from doing what we love, we'll eventually go crazy."

Gretchen's looking at me like maybe I'm crazy. "Did she sing again?"

"She did. But she made me promise to tell her if she sounded like a frog. I'm petrified of frogs, so I told her if I got up and ran, she'd know what her brother said was true."

Gretchen is smiling but hasn't said anything about joining us. A voice inside me says, *it's no big deal, you have enough people.* Another voice instantly overrides it—*it's not about that.* "Would you like to be mine and Traci's personal assistant?"

"What's a personal assistant?"

"It's someone very important who takes care of all the things her boss doesn't have time for." *The brilliant ideas just keep coming!* "You know, Gretchen, we really need a personal assistant. And, you'll be hearing all the songs, so if you decide you want to sing, you can join us at any time."

"I wanna do that," says Gretchen, almost excited.

"Thank you so much! Your first job is to put this list in that sparkly blue bag I accidently left over there on the ground."

"That's easy," Gretchen says, eagerly running off to take care of her first assignment.

"Being our personal assistant is an essential job—not necessarily a difficult one," I laugh, grabbing her hand.

*** 7 ***

"We can do this, right?" I ask Traci.

"Absolutely!" Traci looks at me and cracks up. "Do you feel like I do?"

"I'm on an energy high one second, and then five seconds later I feel like I might collapse."

"Exactly. By the way, how did you talk Gretchen into joining us?"

"It was easy."

"Really? She usually keeps to herself. I was surprised she was here at all." Traci gives me a "what gives" look.

"I just told her a story about a little girl and a frog."

"Like a true story?"

"It's definitely probably true for someone. And we have our very own personal assistant."

Traci smiles and addresses everyone. "Okay, whoever wants to work on signs and bulletins—over here. Everyone who wants to sing and dance, go see Kristi Kate."

To make life easier, on my mad dash to Traci's house, I revised my original script. I cut out all the minor characters and added the role of a Narrator. The Narrator will weave dialogue around the songs so that everything makes sense. (At least it made sense in my mind.) Traci and I will alternate being the Narrator. As far as the actual dialogue… I haven't gotten that far.

After we've gone over the songs a few times, Traci suggests we take our show to the stage. "She's right," I say. "We need to work on some blocking."

"What's blocking?" asks Rachel, running to the stage.

"Don't worry. It sounds more complicated than it is." However… it ended up being a little more complicated than I expected. "Okay, let's take it from the top."

Timmy tosses his hat in the air. "Again?"

"Just one more time," I reassure him. "We've almost got it."

"I'm hungry," says Rachel.

"Are y'all gonna sing this time?" asks Robin.

"We don't wanna take up any more of your time," Traci answers. "We'll practice later."

"Come on! No fair!" yells our cast.

"We can do it," I whisper to Traci.

"I know," Traci whispers back confidently.

And through my big smile, "What are we doing?"

"Not sure. You know "Amazing Grace"?"

"We're definitely going to need that."

Traci laughs through her pasted on smile. "The song!"

"You lead. I'll figure it out."

"We'll do one song," says Traci. "If we do more, it will be dark by the time we're done, and we'll all be in trouble."

"Alright, Creators of Atmosphere (that's what I'm calling our non-performers), you're our audience. Everyone else on stage. And don't forget—if you mess up, don't freak out. Just keep smiling and keep going."

"That goes double for us," Traci whispers, as we begin.

The applause from our "audience" really did the trick—our cast is pumped.

"Check it," says Cameron, showing us the super cool signs he and Jesse made.

"Ask her which one she likes better," commands Jesse.

They have ten options. "Why don't we use all of them," Gretchen suggests.

"Excellent idea." (Excellent, because I can see an argument in the making over this.)

"Look what we did," says Courtney, bringing my attention to a piece of poster board that says *Sign-Up Now To Teach Your Talent!!!!!*

"The glitter exclamation points are a real attention grabber," I smile. "And Todd, you saved us today.

Thanks again." (After Todd called his parents, he "decided" he would sing—I made sure we saved everything even remotely heavy for him to move.)

"Let's meet tomorrow at 11:00," suggests Traci.

"I thought the show was at 7:00?" questions Cameron. "That's what we put on the signs."

"It is," I assure him. We'll rehearse until around 3:00, then take a long break, and be ready-to-go by 7:00."

"What are we wearing?" asks Courtney.

"We don't have to wear those long ugly choir robes do we?" asks Timmy.

"I don't think so," Traci says, giving me a *do they* look.

"Whatever you feel the most comfortable in will be perfect."

As soon as everyone's gone, Traci turns to me. "I think we're going to pull this off."

"Did you hear how amazing we sounded?" I grab Traci's hands and we spin in circles until we collapse. The last rays of sunlight are shining on the cross, making diamonds dance all over the walls. It's like I'm inside one of those prism things I used to play with. I lie here, watching my dreams swim around me. Then all of a sudden, a serious question interrupts me. "What are we wearing?"

"Holy cow!" Traci says, flying to her feet. "I'll call mom and tell her we're on the way home."

As soon as we race out the door, I realize I left my—Traci's jacket. "I'll be right back." Unfortunately, I can't remember where I left it. I finally see it folded nicely on a chair to the left of the stage. *That's weird.* Underneath the jacket is an open Bible. Ephesians 2: 7-10 is highlighted.

> *Now God has us where He wants us, with all the time in this world and the next to shower grace and kindness upon us in Christ Jesus. Saving us is all His idea and all His work. All we have to do is trust Him enough to let Him do it. It's God's gift from start to finish.*

We don't play the major role, if we did,
we'd probably be going around bragging
that we'd done the whole thing! No,
we neither make nor save ourselves.
He creates each of us by Christ Jesus
to join Him in the work He has gotten
ready for us to do. Work He created
us for, even before time began. Work
we'd better be doing.

Hand written in the corner is "See Jeremiah 29:11." I flip through the pages looking for a Jeremiah… *For I know the plans I have for you. Plans to prosper, not to harm, plans to give you a hope and a future.*

"Kristi Kate?" Traci yells.

"Coming." I wonder whose Bible this is. They took the time to make notes, yet the "Belongs to" space is blank.

Traci peeks her head in. "What's up?"

"Nothing," I say, joining her. "Did you see a Bible sitting on that chair earlier?"

"No," Traci answers nonchalantly. "But we've been moving things around all day."

Right. "So what did your mom say about my gorgeous pink ensemble?"

"Well," Traci hesitates. "She's going to try…"

"Don't worry. I'm not getting my hopes up."

Traci looks relived. "I don't have anything as amazing as your pink outfit, but you're welcome to anything I have."

"I'm sure I'll love your clothes. I'm just glad we're the same size."

When we walk into Traci's house, my mom is sitting at the table. *What…*

"I was standing in line at the grocery," Mom explains, "and Jackie was talking to the cashier about the show her daughter was putting on…"

"How cool!" Traci interjects.

It is cool, but it's weird. It's… I don't know what it is.

"So, I introduced myself," Mom explains.

"I told her since my daughter was spending the

night at her borrowed house, the least I could do was give her a ride home," Jackie says.

"Then she mentioned baking cookies," Mom confesses. "And here I am."

Mom does have has a major weakness for cookies.

"Are all those tins full?" asks Traci.

"Yep," Jackie answers, taking a cookie sheet out of the oven.

"Awesome. We can sell them," says Traci.

Traci's mom smiles, "Such an entrepreneur."

"There's enough for us though, right?" I ask, forgetting about the weirdness of this situation and reaching for one.

"Sorry," says Mom.

"It's okay," Traci says. "Thanks for making them. It was a great idea."

Stunned, I put my cookie back. "Yeah, thanks," I mumble.

Mom walks over and puts her hand on my forehead (like she does when I tell her I'm about to die of a heat stroke). "Do you really think we'd forget to make the stars of the show, to us at least, their own personal stash of chocolate chip, peanut butter, and oatmeal cookies?"

"No," I exclaim, taking two. "But I think today has been crazy enough for you not to remember."

"It has been an interesting one," Mom nods.

Jackie takes a seat. "And we want all the details."

Since our mouths are busy, we try and answer their questions with our hands. Great. No time to talk. Have to find clothes. Somehow they get this.

"Speaking of clothes, I don't think your outfit is ever going to look exactly like it did before your swim."

I motion that I figured that was the case… sad, but expected it, thanks for trying. I can tell she has no idea what I'm trying to say. Traci interprets, "She's saying…" and repeats exactly what I was motioning. I nod and give Traci a thumbs up.

"I can't promise it will work, but if you don't mind, I'd like to try something," says Jackie.

Personally, I don't ever see it being beautiful again.

"It can't hurt," I laugh. "Have you ever met Delilah? The woman who owns the house we're staying in?"

"Years ago," answers Jackie.

"What was she like?" I ask.

"Hard to describe."

"Try, Mom!" I only saw her that one time," Traci says reminding me. "She was so beautiful."

Jackie thinks for a second. "There's this aura about her. This incredible energy. It's like she's in her own world, but at the same time, she's completely grounded and available."

"I have to meet her," I say.

"We also have to get going," says Mom.

Traci and I panic—*the clothes.* "We'll hurry," I promise.

Traci's room is painted in soft pinks, blues, yellows, and purples, with hints of rainbows shining underneath flashes of bright, vibrant colors. "Your room is fantabulous!"

"Thanks, Mom painted it for me."

Maybe she can do something with my outfit. I follow

Traci to the closet. "It looks like a sunrise and a sunset all at once."

"It reminds me that every day is a new beginning, but that there's always an ending. Sometimes I like endings, and sometimes I hate them."

"Me, too."

"My clothes are a little different," Traci says.

"I love different."

Traci smiles and swings open the closet. And I'm face to face with Major possibilities. "Wow!"

"Girls are you almost ready?" calls Mom.

"Just a minute," we both reply.

Meanwhile, I need more like a lifetime. I've never seen so much beauty in a closet. *Bang! Boom!* "Traci? Where are you?"

Traci crawls out from underneath the bed holding a bag full of miscellaneous merchandise. "I've never worn any of this, but maybe…" Traci throws a multi-colored boa around her neck.

"Love it! But what's the suitcase for?"

"We don't have time to make major decisions

right now," Traci says, whipping items off the hangers and dropping them into the suitcase.

"Genius." I watch Traci shake the pillows out of the pillowcases and fill them with shoes, "Pure genius."

"The only thing is…"

"Ouch!" I cry. Our luxurious luggage feels like a ton of bricks.

"You okay?" asks Traci.

"Fine, just knocked our wardrobe into my leg. Totally worth it though. What's the thing?" I ask, as we half-carry, half-drag everything into the kitchen.

"Uuh…" Traci's thoughts are interrupted.

"You need all of that for one night?" asks Jackie.

"Course not," Traci breathes. "But we don't have time to try anything on."

"Traci had the brilliant idea of taking everything we like. That way we can leave now, and try on later."

"And I guess you like everything in her closet?" asks Mom.

"Oh my gosh, you should see it!"

"It looks like I'm going to. Did you happen to remember we're walking back?"

I did not. "They're not that heavy," I say, willing my brain to believe me.

"How about I drive you over?" offers Jackie.

"For real, Mom? Usually you say I have great legs and to use them."

"I do, and I'll continue to. But this is a special occasion." We breathe a sigh of relief, and Jackie laughs. "Were you really planning on walking?"

"We hadn't gotten that far with our plan yet, but I'm sure we could have done it," I reply, struggling to pick up the suitcase and put it in the trunk.

Moments later we pull into the driveway. "Thanks for the star treatment," Traci smiles, giving her Mom a hug.

"You're welcome. And I have no doubt you would have eventually gotten here on your own."

"Eventually, like tomorrow," I say, thanking her.

I can't wait to show Traci around and try on our

clothes, but… "Mom, do you need help with dinner?" *Please say no.*

I don't know if it's because I tend to make a mess when I'm in the kitchen, or that all I know how to make is pizza, or if she's just reading my mind but…"How about a fashion show instead?"

Look out Hollywood, here we come.

*** 8 ***

"Our very own movie set!" Traci gasps, as I open the door to the pink palace.

It is! "Let's lay the clothes on the bed, and put the accessories on…"

"That lavender love seat," squeals Traci, already opening the suitcase and laying our selections out.

Traci must have a rich relative that sends her clothes from Paris or something. "What a fabulous collection this is," I drawl. (I heard that once on E! It's shimmering fun being able to say it.)

We decide to start on opposite ends and pick one item from each category. "I'll return momentarily." I sneak out with a hot pink summery dress with braided spaghetti straps, a funky lavender and turquoise sheer scarf, and a handful of accessories. I slip on the dress, throw the scarf over my shoulder (so it will flow behind me like I'm walking down the red carpet), and put on a simple pair of drop down diamond earrings, which I sincerely hope aren't real. If they are, there's no way I'm wearing them. (Earrings don't like my ears that much—especially the right one. It's always falling out.) I dress my arms with antique looking bracelets, and top it all off with a pink, heart shaped ring.

I run down to the living room where I left my hot pink platform sandals, that luckily, I didn't swim in. "I'm going for a business sparkly look," I say, running back up the stairs.

"Tada!" Traci says, throwing open the door.

"Oh my stars!" (I've never said that before, but I love the way it sounds), and I LOVE Traci's outfit. Traci's wearing a sea green fitted skirt, a gold belt, and a hot pink top with sheer butterfly petals coming from what would normally be sleeves. I know I'm not describing this well, which is near tragic, for it's the most magnificent and glamorous thing I've ever seen.

"Love, love, love!" we both say at once.

"How did you come up with that?" Traci asks.

"What part of the universe did you get...?"

"My mom made everything," Traci answers.

"Are you serious?" I exclaim.

"Look at you two!" says Mom coming down the hall.

"You like?" I ask.

"Absolutely. You girls look exquisite." Traci and I beam. "But do you think you might be a little dressy for church?"

"I don't think you can be too dressed up for God, Mom."

"I never thought of it that way before. Is everyone else dressing up?"

"We don't know," Traci answers. "Kristi Kate told them to wear whatever they feel most comfortable in—because that's their perfect outfit."

"That sounds like something she'd say," says Mom.

"So, Timmy will probably wear his baseball hat backwards. I don't know why, he just always does," Traci explains.

"Guess that's the way he feels most comfortable," I offer.

Traci agrees. "Courtney will probably wear a long sleeve buttoned up blouse and long pants."

"Ugh, that sounds miserable." Mom gives me a look. (I'm pretty positive it means my perfect is not everyone else's perfect.) "Courtney will look splendid in her buttoned up, hot outfit. If I had a cool body temperature, I'd wear a black velvet coat with a big hood lined in white fur."

"Totally Hollywood!" says Traci.

"Thanks!"

"ANYWAY" Mom says, "If Jackie thinks your outfits are appropriate, it's fine with me."

"I'm sure she will. She made them."

"I'm impressed," says Mom. "I wish I could sew."

"I wish you could too. Maybe you could take a class," I suggest.

"Maybe you could!" she suggests back. "So what's next?"

* * * * * * * * * *

After dinner and a lot of rehearsing, Traci and I crash. Well, Traci does and I want to, but I can't relax until... I hear the old door creek open—*Dad's back.* I crawl out of bed, careful not to wake Traci.

"You look like you've had a day," says Mom.

"What kind airport is closed until sun down on Sunday?" Dad complains.

"We could leave Monday morning," I suggest, coming down the stairs. "Then we won't have to fly at night."

"School? Work?" Dad says, reminding me.

I nod. *Like I could really forget this.* "About tomorrow..."

"I don't want to hear another word about..."

"I'm glad we're going to be here." This catches Dad by surprise, and he forgets to tell me not to interrupt him. (Dad hates being interrupted. Sometimes, I think he'd be fine if I never talked—unless it was to agree with him.)

"Since when?" Dad asks.

"It's a long story..."

"I'm glad you met some friends," Dad says when I finish.

"So you'll come?" I ask, following him into the kitchen. "I'm singing two solos and..."

Dad opens and closes cabinets. He must really want whatever he's looking for, because each time he doesn't find it, he shuts the door with a little more bang. "I agreed to let you help out with those kids at your school, but you know how I feel about..."

"About what?" I ask. An intense sweaty heat explodes in my heart. *I know what.*

Dad slams the refrigerator door. "Your obsession with this whole performing arts thing."

"Don't you think I'd rather play softball, be a

cheerleader, a tennis player… do something—anything that would make you proud of me?"

"It has nothing to do with my being proud of you. I don't want to see you disappointed."

"You're the one disappointing me!"

"Young lady!"

"I keep telling myself that when you see me on stage, you'll get it, you'll… I didn't choose this dream, Dad. It chose me."

A few long seconds go by. "Where is it?" he asks, forcing the words out.

"At the church," I say quietly.

"Not happening."

"What's wrong with church? I used to love going."

"I never told you not to go," Dad shouts, "And now is not the time…"

It's never the time. But there won't be a show tomorrow if I say that out loud. Least not one with me in it.

Back in bed, I stare at the ceiling. Thank goodness Traci's asleep. I'd be so embarrassed if…

"My dad showed up when I was three. He left when I was six."

She heard. "You're awake."

"Yeah," Traci whispers.

"I hate that…" *God, I'm selfish.* "I wondered about your dad. I didn't know if I should ask."

"It's okay."

"You must think I'm such a brat."

"I think your dad should want to come," says Traci.

"And yours should have stayed."

Traci and I stare at the dark ceiling, listening to our own lives. After a while, Traci begins to share bits and pieces with me. Her voice is raspy. Far-away. Almost like she's talking about someone else. I hold on to her every word. Most of all, I listen to what she doesn't say.

"…Mom cried all the time. I thought it was because she missed him and that it was my fault. I packed my suitcase once. I don't know where I was going. When Mom saw me, she said she was crying for me. She blamed herself for him. We started going to church after that." Traci pauses. "I wouldn't want anyone to go through what we did. But I want everyone to know God like we do."

I wipe my eyes with the end of the pillowcase. "Do you think it was God's plan that it happened?" I sniffle. "So you could find Him?"

"No. But God does have plans to prosper us," says Traci. And if we give Him all the bad stuff, He'll use it for our good."

"I should be writing this down," I mumble, searching in the dark for my diary.

"It's in the Bible," Traci laughs.

"Oh," I say, feeling not so smart. "You know how the Bible says that God knew us before time began? And that He has a special purpose and plan for our life?"

"Uh-huh," Traci yawns.

"I've been thinking about that all afternoon."

"All afternoon?"

"Not all afternoon. But it's been in the back of my

head… It sounds like God gave us—I mean, created us, with specific gifts and talents for a reason. Like there's a bigger picture. What do you think?" For a second, I think Traci's in deep thought. "Night, Traci," I say softly.

Life would be so different if…

*** 9 ***

As soon as I see Traci's eyelids flutter, I scoot out from behind the desk. "Finally! You're awake."

Traci rubs her eyes. "Kind of."

"Can you play the piano?" *Please say you play by ear.*

Traci gives me a why-does-this matter-right-now look and pulls the covers over her head.

"I had this dream last night," I explain. "But it was more than a dream."

"We can't afford... I haven't taken any lessons." Traci sticks her head out. "But I know I'm meant to play, because if I really like a song, I can play it within a couple minutes."

I hand her my diary. "Do you like this?"

"Sing it for me," Traci says, instantly awake.

"Well, it's kind of a couple different songs all put together." Traci nods like she already knows this, and that I should start singing. So I do. But after a second, she closes her eyes, so I stop.

"Keep going," she urges, "I'm visualizing."

"Oh, I thought you..."

"No talking," says Traci. "Just sing."

So, I sing. And Traci lies there, waving her hands back and forth, tapping the pillow in different rhythms—*visualizing*. Over and over, I sing, until...

"This is part of God's plan," proclaims Traci, popping out of bed.

"I think so too," I exclaim. "But how do you know?"

"When you're tight with God—when you know His ways, and pray and stuff," says Traci, throwing on clothes, "you know if something is a God idea, a good idea, or a my-mind-was-in-the-wrong-place idea. But hurry," she says, looking at me standing still. "God ideas take a lot of work."

I scribble Mom a note. "Ready."

By the time the others get there, Traci and I are on it. "Little change in plans," Traci announces. "Don't freak out, we just learned everything yesterday." Every kid gives Traci and me an *exactly* look. "So," Traci continues, "how hard can it be to unlearn it?"

"This happens all the time on Broadway," I explain. "The directors get brainstorms the night before the show. Some of the performers can't take it, but the real ones… they thrive."

"We're not on Broadway," Todd reminds me.

"True. But I'm going to be one day and I need the practice. But you're right," I sigh. "Maybe it's too much."

"No it's not!" says Courtney.

"Am I still rappin?" asks Tyrell.

"What does a brainstorm feel like?" asks Timmy.

"I might wanna be on Broadway!" exclaims Rachel.

"Traci?" I ask. Traci answers by taking a seat at the piano. "This is what we're thinking: When Traci hits that note, the dancers will come in. Same places as yesterday, but forget the choreography. Let the music lead you. Everyone will join me on the chorus…"

A couple hours later, it's unanimous—this is it! "Let's take a quick lunch break."

Robin looks petrified. "What if…"

"You won't forget anything," I assure her.

"Should I tell everyone to be back in thirty minutes?" whispers Gretchen (who's been right by our side all morning).

"What would we do without you?" I ask, giving her the go-ahead. *I wonder if she'd like to come home with me.*

"You're rockin up there," says a rather big man.

"Thanks," says Traci, startled.

I offer my hand. "I'm Kristi Kate."

"This is Todd's dad," says Traci.

"Forgive my manners—name's Ryan."

"Nice to meet you." Ryan nods and… just stands there.

"Drums and a little bass would…"

"Do you play?" I ask.

"Fool around a little." Ryan talks to the ground, "Always wanted to do something with it, but…"

"Now's your chance!" Traci says, jumping in.

"I wouldn't wanna mess with your show," Ryan says seriously. "What you're doing…" he looks us in the eyes, "It's pretty great."

"We're just the vessels," says Traci.

I've got to learn this lingo. "I'm pretty positive you're supposed to play the drums, the bass, whatever you want. And if you have any friends that can be here within the hour, bring them on," I add.

"Well, alrighty then." Ryan turns to go, "Todd might not be into it though."

Traci and I swallow our laughter. That's the understatement of the century. "We'll take care of it," I smile. Ryan nods gratefully and scurries off.

Traci looks at me. "God ideas are…"

"Incredible."

When everyone's back on stage, Traci shares our latest development. "Every show needs a guest star…"

"I thought Kristi Kate was the guest star," questions Gretchen.

I love this child. "Traci's talking about Ryan, Todd's dad," I say, giving Gretchen a thank-you-for-thinking-of-me smile.

All eyes are gawking on Todd, as his dad shuffles to the stage. "He's not bad," Todd shrugs. (We caught up with Todd on the break. It wasn't as tragic as we had expected.)

"Hey!" calls a guy with a beard almost down to his knees.

Ryan waves. "Up here, Bowie."

Bowie turns back to the door. "Yep. This is the place, come on in."

I hate when people judge me by my looks. And I pride myself on not doing it. But…

"I've never seen these people before," whispers Traci.

"It's like we're making history or something," I breathe.

Traci leaps off the stage. "Let us help you."

"The word's out, we're hot," I say, to our somewhat shocked cast. "Everyone wants to perform with us."

"Are we like gonna have a whole band?" asks Timmy.

"That's what it looks like." Adrenaline rushes through my entire being. "Let's take it from the top!"

By mid-afternoon, we are Broadway!!! And *Believe* is mere hours away. Traci and I had planned on getting ready together but, "Do you think it will be faster if…" Traci starts.

"Can you pick us up?" I ask, already running up the hill that feels so familiar now.

"See you soon," Traci answers, taking a left.

★★★★★★★★★★★

I'm lying on the bed, fully dressed and ready to go, when Mom steps into the pink palace.

"This room was made for you."

I know.

"You look stunning," Mom says when I don't say anything.

"Thanks." *Part of me feels stunning. The other part,* "Any chance…"

Mom shakes her head. "I tried."

I tell Mom it's okay. Even though we both know it's not. "I've experienced more emotions in the last forty eight hours than I have in my entire life." Mom sits down on the bed and takes my hand. "I'm sorry I accused you of not understanding the other day. There was something I hadn't told you about the show. I worked so hard and thought it was my only chance to…"

Mom passes me a tissue. I dab my eyes and blow my nose, trying not to mess up the little bit of makeup she let me put on. "Hopefully I'll get all my tears out before I'm an official teenager and get to wear makeup all the time."

Mom shakes her head. "It's why they invented water proof mascara."

"I'm only buying that kind."

Mom smiles. "There will be more tears. And as long as you don't give up, there will always be another chance."

"You have no idea." I want to tell Mom everything, but—I tell her I'll be down in five. I need a second to just be still.

I run my hands across the silky bedspread and close my eyes. I wish I could thank Delilah and her granddaughter for letting me stay, *live,* for at least a moment here. *I'm going to miss Traci so much.* She was praying for a friend like me, when really, I should have been praying for a friend like her. For some reason, Ryan and Bowie flash across my heart. *They're so brave.* Which reminds me, I have to go back and brave another year at school with no one knowing, no one understanding. *It might be the same, but I'm not.* I'm not exactly sure what that means, but it's true. All of a sudden, the uninvited truth, that I'm desperately trying not to think about, throws itself in my face. *He's not coming.* How can I...

"They're here," calls Mom.

The Dream God gave me. And the one He made me for. That's how I can.

✦✦✦ 10 ✦✦✦

Traci and I are taking selfies, when rays of light blast into the car. "What's going on?" asks Traci. "I have no idea," marvels Jackie.

The closer we get to the church, the brighter the sky gets. "Maybe it's the media!" I cheer. Then I look at Traci's face—they don't even have a gym. "I forgot," I say, disappointed. I remind myself that it's not about me anyway but...

"It's not bad to want to be a star," Traci says, sensing the dilemma in my heart. "The world needs good role models."

I squeeze Traci's hand. "I love you!"

"Wow," Mom exclaims, as we pull into the parking lot. Traci and I are speechless—the beaming lights are coming from a huge banner hung across the church. *Believe!* sparkles like zillions of strobe lights strung together, it's... it's sheer radiance.

"I think your whole town is here," I say, half freaking out and half buzzing like a bee.

"This is our town plus a hundred people," Traci breathes.

"Did you expect this kind of turnout?" Mom asks.

"No!" Traci and I both scream.

"This is exciting. But it's going to take a while to find parking," Jackie says, opening the door. "I'll meet you inside."

I hear Mom talking to Jackie. Traci hops out and holds the door open for me—but my legs won't move. "Are you okay?" she whispers.

"Excuse me, Traci," Mom says, sticking her head back in the car. "Kristi Kate, you've wanted this your entire life. Now, snap out of it."

"Sorry," I say scrambling out. "Thanks, Mom."

"You're welcome," Mom says, marching ahead of us. "Wait. Why am I leading the way? I have no idea where I'm going." This makes us laugh—which feels really good.

Meanwhile, everyone is raving about the banner, but no one knows who did it. One thing is for sure; it's breathtaking and must have cost a fortune.

"I didn't expect this," I whisper to Mom, my knees shaking.

"The crowd or your nerves?" Mom asks.

I laugh and choke at the same time. "Neither."

"Look at me," Mom says gently. "I don't always know how to encourage you, but… You were made for this."

"You're going to love the show," I say, brushing away a tear.

"I know," says Mom.

"I mean like you really will."

"Everybody! Over here," shouts Traci.

I give Mom a hug and run over. After a few seconds of extreme excitement, we take each other's hand and bow our heads.

"Okay if I join?" asks Bowie.

"Of course!" Traci says.

"We're just not used to telling adults what to do," I say apologizing. And with that, Bowie and the rest of his crew come into our circle. *God ideas are beautiful.*

After praying, I ask everyone to stay for a second longer. "I want to thank each and every one of you. The emergency landing we made... well, it's the best thing that's ever happened to me."

"Are you like practicing for an Academy Award or something?" asks Timmy.

"No!" *But I should.*

Moments later, we take our places on the dark stage. The band, *our band*, plays the intro to *Believe*. The spotlight finds me. I catch a glimpse of Traci's awed face at the piano, and begin...

Kirstin Leigh

"All this time
Been fighting lies
No one could understand
Laughing at my dreams,
Still this beat in my heart
Longs to believe
In all You have for me"

Overhead lights follow each dancer as they twirl across the stage. The drums get louder, the guitars kick in and the violin revs up for the chorus, and everyone sings…

"Gotta Believe,
Gotta be a reason
For this dream
Inside of me
Gotta believe
Gotta be a reason
For you,
For me
In what I can not see
I gotta believe"

"Gotta Believe," flows into "Dream Through Me."
Traci steps away from the piano and takes center stage.

(Traci)

"So dream through me
Make me all I can be
Dream through me
Want the world to see"

(Kristi Kate)

"Your dream in me
The reason I'm here
Your dream in me
I shall not fear"

(Kristi Kate & Traci harmonize)

"Won't let the world
Tell me how to be
Only You know
Your Plan for me"

(Everyone)

"Plans to prosper, not to harm
Oh, yeah, I'm safe in Your arms

So Dream through me
Make me all I can be
Your purpose, Your plan
Make me all that I am
Your dream in me
The reason I'm here
Your dream in me, I shall not fear"

Spotlights flicker and flash on singers, dancers and musicians...

(Robin & Rachel)

"So dream through me… I'm ready now
Dream through me… I'm ready now"

(Everyone)

"We're ready now.... we're ready nowwwwwww"

Music transitions into "Time for a Change." Timmy comes out rapping (with his hat on backwards).

(Timmy)

"We can make a difference
You and me
When we embrace who we are
We'll find harmony"

(Tyrell)

"You're one of a kind
And I am too
Gotta use the gifts,
He gave me and you"

(Timmy)

"Created for His purpose
Designed for His plan
But we gotta come together
Time to take a stand"

Rap transitions into "As One." Everyone unites and sings…

> *"As one, you and me*
> *Living life in harmony*
> *As one, what the world can be*
> *But it begins with His dream*
> *Inside of me"*

Music reverts back to "Dream Through Me." Same melody but with more groove.

> *"So dream through me*
> *Make me all I can be*
> *Dream through me*
> *Want the world to see*
> *Your dream in me*
>
> *Your dream in me*
> *The reason I'm here*
> *Your dream in me*
> *I shall not fear*
>
> *Your dream in me I gotta believe*
> *Your dream in me sets me free"*

(add-libs & repeats)

"Dream through me… I'm ready now…"

Applause ricochets against the walls. We take our bows, but it doesn't stop. None of us know what to do. Then Ryan catches my eye—he's going into the chorus of "Gotta Believe." I nod and he knows I'm with him.

"Gotta Believe,
Gotta be a reason
For this dream
Inside of me
Gotta believe
Gotta be a reason"

I motion for everyone to join me…

"For you,
For me
In what I can not see
Gotta believe…"

We sing it through a couple more times, before the symbols crash in that beautiful *this is what I want for my life,* kind of clang. The entire congregation is on their feet, cheering.

"I've gotta pee," Timmy whispers. I nod and laugh while smiling. Right when I think I can't smile anymore, Mr. Johnson (an elder or deacon I think), takes the stage. Traci and I move over to where the band is, while the rest of our cast joins their parents.

Mr. Johnson clears his throat. "As most of you know, I've tried, along with many others, to revive this church. I came tonight out of a sense of obligation. And curiosity. What could a handful of kids do in a day?" Mr. Johnson pauses. "I got my answer—a whole lot. Betsy, can you bring me the sign in sheet?" Mr. Johnson takes a second to study it. "You youngsters raised over $900 tonight."

"Are you serious?" yells Todd.

"I am," says Mr. Johnson. "Forty-three people are here tonight for the first time." I steal a glance at Ryan. There's a light in his eyes, I didn't notice before. He catches me staring at him and does a *boombababboom* thing on the drums. Mr. Johnson keeps talking through the applause. He looks a little like a shock victim. "Thirteen people signed up to teach various classes and activities… Bible school, softball, basketball, creative writing, adult education, marriage counseling…" Mr. Johnson rubs his eyes. "With all this in place, we should have no problem finding a full time Pastor." I grab Traci's hand—this is unbelievable. "However, it might take a bit, and I don't want to lose what we have right now. Is there anyone who can head up a praise and worship team?"

And before I even know what's happening…"Traci can," pops right out of my mouth. Mr. Johnson gives me a who-are-you-again look. *Maybe I'm not supposed to vote since I don't live here.*

Mr. Johnson smiles at Traci. "You did a tremendous job tonight. But this position will require serious dedication and discipline. You're a little young for all that."

Mr. Johnson waits for Traci to agree, but she's frozen—like one of those mannequins in a store window. I hope she's not mad. She doesn't necessarily look mad—just stunned. I really think once she comes alive again she'll be totally into this. So, for now...

"I agree she's young, Mr. Johnson. But I think that works to her benefit. Traci identifies with the kids, since she still kind of is one. She also babysits for many of the families here, which shows she's trusted and responsible." Mr. Johnsons face is going in and out of focus, and I can hear my voice, but I have no idea what I'm saying. *I wonder if I'm having an out of body experience.* "The ability to work individually, as well as with a team are very important aspects of any leader. Traci proved tonight that she has these qualities. She also has a true heart for God and everyone here," I conclude. My heart sounds like Ryan's drums.

"I'm sorry dear, what is your name again?"

"Kristi Kate, Sir."

"Are you Traci's agent?" Mr. Johnson laughs nicely.

"No, Sir, she's my friend. My best friend."

"I can do this," Traci says, alive and confident. *Yes! She's back.* "I just need to ask my mom if it's okay first."

A few people laugh—everyone looks at Traci's mom. "I personally nominate my daughter for this trial position," Jackie says, standing up. "Trial, meaning that if her school work starts to fail, or I see it being too much for her, we can re-evaluate. But for now, I'd like her to have the opportunity to try."

"All those in favor of Traci leading the worship team, please stand," says Mr. Johnson. There it goes… another round of applause. Traci and I look at each other. *How did all this happen?* A God idea. A God Dream.

I watch our band packing up, wishing this night could last forever. "Thanks for letting me play," says a girl with long braids who played the violin. "I think it might have changed my life."

My throat feels like I swallowed a wad of glue.

(And only by sheer will power do I not burst into tears.) Traci on the other hand… "Any chance you'd like to do "change your life" type things weekly?"

A second goes by. "I think she's asking if you'd like to play every week," I offer.

"I would love it if you could," Traci confirms.

A million emotions swim across our new friend's face. "I'd like that. I'd really that," she says, her braids swinging from side to side. "I'm Penny, by the way."

"There's a bunch of people who want to say congratulations," says Gretchen coming up on stage.

Traci gives Penny her number, "We'll talk soon."

I pick Gretchen up in a victory pose and wave bye to Penny. After a million hugs, thank yous and good-byes we're almost ready to go, when I see Timmy sneaking off. "Hold up! I laugh, running over. "I need a hug from my favorite rapper."

"Oh, Geez," Timmy sighs, trying not to smile. Reluctantly, he lets me hug him. And that's when I see it—there's gold dust on his face. "Did you make that beautiful banner?"

"Sort of."

"Why didn't you say anything? It's spectacular!" Timmy shrugs. "How? How did you do it? What kind of lights are those anyway? Did you know you can see them from miles away?" Timmy looks dizzy— probably because I just asked him ten questions at once. "Sorry, I'm going to be quiet now."

Timmy takes a big breath. "See, my brother loves lights…"

I met his brother earlier. He's in a wheel chair and had to be carried in from the back because the church doesn't have one of those ramp things. *It doesn't have one yet.*

"He plays with them all the time," Timmy continues. "Well, he says he's not playing. He says he's doing research."

"I completely understand."

"He's always trying to get them to shine brighter and farther. They look cool, right?"

"I've never seen anything so amazing. Where is

he?" I ask, searching the crowd. "I want to tell him what a genius he is."

"I'll go get him."

"I'll wait right here," I promise, waving Traci over. "I found out who did the masterpiece outside."

"No!" says Traci excited.

"Yes. And here he comes."

Rob, Timmy's brother is way nice and seems glad he was "found out." He explains the lights to us, but the only part of it I understand is that he has phenomenal brain cells.

Rob continues. "And then Timmy held the banner while Mom climbed up the ladder, and I wheeled back and forth shouting out instructions."

"That's awesome!" we exclaim.

"Girls?" Mom calls. "Jackie's waiting on us."

Traci and I give Rob a hug and then make our way out. "You're for sure, for sure coming to visit, right?" I ask.

"Before Christmas."

I slump in the car. "That sounds forever away."

Traci nods and bites her lip. "How is it possible to be so happy and so sad at the same time?"

"I don't know," Traci struggles.

"Omygosh," I laugh. "My brain is spinning. I didn't even realize I said that out loud."

"I'm going to miss you so much," Traci chokes.

"Thank goodness you were bored and decided to come over and introduce yourself."

"I can't imagine if I hadn't."

"Me either."

"We're here," says Mom tenderly.

Traci hands me a box wrapped in shiny pink paper. "This is from Mom and me."

"But I didn't get you anything."

"Yes, you did," says Jackie.

"You got me a job!" Traci exclaims, making us burst into laughter. It's the kind of laughter that changes into tears if you're not careful. The kind that sounds bizarre to anyone who's not in the moment. After a few more seconds, Dad turns on the propeller—a sign that it's past time for us to be in the plane. Traci and I know that "good-bye" is not in our future. "See you soon."

"See you soon," Traci smiles.

"Call me tomorrow," I yell through the wind, as Mom pushes me into the plane.

I buckle my seat-belt and watch Traci wave, the *Believe!* sign glowing in the background. I reach for Mom's hand and say a prayer for a safe flight home. *Why can't we all just live next door to each other?*

★★★★★★★★★★★

Mom gently shakes my shoulders. "Honey, are you going to sleep in the car?"

"Hmm?" I mumble.

"We're home." I blink my eyes a couple of times. "You fell asleep before we even took off," Mom explains. "Dad carried you from the plane to the car."

I don't know how I feel about that. I stumble out of the car and into the house. "You should have woken me up." I'm half-way to my room when...

"I heard I missed a great show," says Dad.

What? "You did," I choke.

"I should have come. And I'm sorry."

Just when you've talked yourself out of wanting something...

"For what it's worth, I'm proud of you."

You realize how much you need it. I lean against the balcony—my heart and head in a tug-of-war. Slowly, I move down the stairs and into Dad's arms. "It's worth a lot." I rest my head against Dad's shoulder, knowing I can't hold the tears back any longer. *Does this mean?*

There's only one thing I know for sure... You've just gotta Believe.

P.S.

I carefully un-wrap my gift, never expecting... My outfit! Jackie redesigned it for me. She took off the once fur, turned wet chicken feather sleeves, and cut the neckline to make it off the shoulder, then lined the whole thing with small iridescent sequins. She added to the miniskirt (it had become), a sheer purple material thing, and cut it in a slant like the top. It has tiny pink, purple and turquoise flowers embedded into the material. At the bottom of it, she placed a piece of the original pink satin. It's perfect.

Kirstin Leigh grew up in a tiny town in Kentucky, where she had lots of time to dream big. Kirstin got a job when she was twelve years old and told everyone she was saving her money to move to New York City. Which is exactly what she did.

Kirstin's written countless articles for national publications and for International author and life coach, Tim Storey's Superrifickid's site. She's sings at churches, ceremonies, special events, toured with a top 40 band, and recorded her first CD with Grammy Award Winner, Tim Miner.

Kirstin's breakout book for adults and teens, "Change Your Story," is now available on Amazon. Her new song, "Changed My Story," recorded with Grammy Award Winner, Brian Yaskulka, is available on Spotify, ITunes, CDBaby, and Kirstin's website: Kirstinleigh.biz.

Believe is the first book in the Kristi Kate series.

To find out about Kirstin's latest projects or to have her speak and sing at your next event, visit Kirstinleigh.biz

You can also follow Kirstin on:

instagram.com/KirstinLeigh3
facebook.com/KirstinLeighWriter
twitter.com/KirstinLeigh3

Made in the USA
Columbia, SC
01 November 2018